"You are looking very beautiful, Sara."

"No...please, no!" Sara's startled cry as his hand moved to explore her exposed breast was smothered by Jabir's descending mouth, warm and firm. Sara felt as though she was drowning in feelings she didn't know existed.

As Jabir took his hands from her body, Sara scrambled to cover herself. Jabir gave a dry bark of laughter.

"There was one subject we didn't discuss—the perfectly normal bodily functions between consenting adults." Sara was looking at him in dawning horror. "I suggest we leave this distressing subject...for the time being," Jabir said as he turned to leave.

Left alone, Sara gave way to tears. How could she face intimacy with this man who didn't love or even particularly care for her...?

MARY LYONS

desire in the desert

Harlequin Books

TORONTO • NEW YORK • LONDON
AMSTERDAM • PARIS • SYDNEY • HAMBURG
STOCKHOLM • ATHENS • TOKYO • MILAN

Harlequin Presents first edition June 1984
ISBN 0-373-10701-3

Original hardcover edition published in 1984
by Mills & Boon Limited

CHAPTER ONE

SARA glanced down at the large diamond ring flashing on her finger, at the mink coat draped across the seat beside her, and then looked across the cabin of the luxuriously furnished aeroplane, at her husband. He was sitting at a desk, signing documents and issuing orders to his assistant, John Morgan.

Her *husband*! Sara leaned back in the leather armchair and sighed. It was all so unbelievable! Never in her wildest flight of fancy could she have ever imagined ... Why, she hadn't even met Jabir until a month ago. The last two weeks had seemed like a dream—an Arabian Nights dream, she thought wryly, as she glanced again at the man she had married that morning: Prince Jabir Ibn Abdul al Shakir.

'We'll be landing in an hour's time at Nice airport, *madame*.' The French stewardess smiled down at Sara. 'Is there anything you would like to drink? Tea or coffee, perhaps?'

'Oh, tea, please,' said Sara, and as the girl disappeared into the galley behind her, looked around the main saloon of the private jet owned by her new husband. She had flown often enough in the past, but never, never in anything like this. Wide, comfortable white leather armchairs, containing the regulation seatbelts, were grouped in the sitting area, while the forward end of the saloon was obviously the 'office'. It contained two desks, the one Jabir sat at, and another for his assistant sited next to the telephones and a telex machine.

The stewardess set a tea tray down on the table in front of her. Sara sipped the warm liquid, and gazed over at her husband absorbed by the papers before him. That was how she had first met him, she remembered;

just four short weeks ago. She knew, of course, that they had an Arab prince staying at the hotel, but she knew nothing more about him, until one of the receptionists rang through to her father's office.

'Sorry to bother you, Sara, but Prince Jabir's just rung down from the Rumanian Suite. He wants to see your father, right away.'

'Well, he can't,' said Sara, busy with the hotel accounts. 'Dad's away for the day, playing golf in Kent.'

'Look, Sara, I think you'd better go and see him. He made it sound quite urgent,' the receptionist said, adding, 'It wasn't just a request, it sounded more like a command. He does stay here a lot when he's in London . . .'

'All right,' Sara sighed, 'I'll go up and see what he wants straight away.' But it was over an hour later before she stood outside the door of the suite, brushing a tired hand over her long honey-coloured hair.

What a day! On the way to the lift, she had glanced into the Balkan Room, to check that everything was ready for the oil company's cocktail party that evening. Nothing had been done, as had happened all too often lately, and she had spent some considerable time chasing up the manager, and directing the necessary work. Useless man, she had thought, as the lift rose to the top floor. Why does Dad keep him on? As she stepped out of the lift, she was waylaid by he housekeeper who complained, as usual, about the urgent need to replace much of the hotel linen. It was all so depressing, she thought, as she waited for her knock to be answered. The hotel seemed to be sliding further and further into financial disaster, and there was nothing she could do about it.

The door of the suite was opened by a man in Arab dress, who bowed and gestured her forward, through a small lobby, into a large lounge whose only occupant, a man, was sitting at the far end of the room behind a large desk.

'Prince Jabir?' she queried in a surprised tone.

The man looked up. 'Can I help you?' he said with one eyebrow raised as he stared at the girl across the room.

Sara stood staring back at him as she tried, rapidly, to re-assess her previously formed ideas about Arab princes. From his immaculately styled black hair, tipped with silver at the temples, her eyes ran over his dark suit, pale shirt and striped tie. No flowing robes, no head-covering; even his skin isn't dark, she thought, just creamy, as if he had been in the sun for a few days. Her gaze moved from his firm mouth to the high cheekbones, and met his eyes staring at her with the same frank appraisal as her own. The gleam in his hooded dark eyes had a disturbing quality, and she blushed as she replied nervously, 'You rang for me?'

'I am almost certain—in fact I am sure that I did not,' he said in a strong, firm voice.

'I'm sorry . . . I'm sorry . . .' Sara was flustered by the Prince's unexpected public school accent, and finding it awkward to be under such an intense scrutiny from those hooded dark eyes.

'There's no need to be sorry, Miss . . .? What can I do for you?'

'Miss Morrison—Sara Morrison . . . er . . . er . . . Prince.' Sara was furious with herself. She was normally cool, calm and collected—what was wrong with her today? What did it matter that she didn't know how to address an Arab prince? There was no need to stutter like a schoolgirl, was there? She blushed as she caught an amused gleam in the dark eyes regarding her, and tried to pull herself together.

'My father . . . I believe you wanted to see my father. I'm afraid he's . . . he's away at a meeting just at the moment.' She no longer felt guilty at having to lie about her father's absences from the hotel, she'd been doing it for so long that the evasion leapt with familiarity to her lips.

'The receptionist tells me that you have a problem. Can I help you in any way?' she added.

The Prince rose, and walked over to a group of deep easy chairs. 'It was very good of you to come and see me, Miss ... er ... Miss Morrison. Please sit down.'

Until he stood up, she hadn't realised just how large the prince was. Well over six feet, with broad shoulders, his tall slim figure dominated the room. Sara, in a way she couldn't define, felt nervous and ill at ease.

'If you could just tell me what the problem is ...?' she said in a nervous rush. 'I'm sure you must be busy, and ...'

'Please, sit down,' the Prince repeated, and it was clearly an order, not a request.

Ruffled at not being in control of the situation, Sara sank down in the chair indicated by the Prince, trying to think what could have gone wrong. It's probably the bathwater, she thought gloomily; there had been lots of complaints about it already this week.

The Prince's voice cut through her thoughts. 'You mentioned your father ...'

'Yes. My father is James Morrison. He—he owns this hotel. If there's anything—anything that I can do—I'm sure when he returns, he'll ...' Her voice died away.

'Yes, I wish to speak to him about this hotel.' The prince rested his elbows on the arms of his chair, slowly rotating a heavy gold ring on the little finger of his hand. The seconds slipped by as he regarded her intently in silence.

Under his gaze, Sara flushed and shifted uneasily in her chair. She found his air of authority and command disturbing and wished, quite illogically, that she was wearing something smarter than the grey suit and white blouse she habitually wore during working hours.

She needn't have worried. The classical suit together with the blouse, tied in a bow at the neck, set off her figure admirably, and her long straight blonde hair, flushed cheeks and startling blue eyes, all combined to present a picture of a beautiful woman.

The Prince broke the strained silence. 'Tell me about this hotel, Miss Morrison.'

'The hotel?' Sara looked at him bewildered.

'Yes. Does your father own it all himself, for instance, or are other members of your family involved?'

'Really, Prince! I'm—I'm just here to see if I can deal with any complaint you may have. Not . . . not . . .'

'We will come to my "complaint" later, if you please,' he said firmly. 'I am staying in this hotel, which is, I must say, managed very unsatisfactorily. I wish to know more about the management.'

Sara flushed with embarrassment at his words. He was quite right, of course. Matters did seem to be going from bad to worse. But he had no right to speak so slightingly of what was, to all intents and purposes, her home. Oh yes, he does, she reminded herself. He's a guest here, after all. She sighed—she'd better tell him what he wanted to know, and get the interview over with as fast as possible.

'My family have owned the Wivern Hotel since 1865,' she said, 'and my father is the sole owner at the present time.' The Prince remained silent, as she continued nervously, 'It's never been a large or important London hotel, it's just our situation, right in the heart of Mayfair, which—well, which our customers find useful. Most of our clients have been country families up for the odd week in London, or visitors from abroad. Like yourself.' Sara gave him a brief smile.

'1865? That was quite a time ago, surely?' he prompted.

Sara shrugged. 'I don't know much about the early days, really. I suppose the peak of the hotel's prosperity was at the turn of the century, before the First World War. Many of the old nobility from what's now the Eastern satellite countries of Russia used to stay here. Hence the Balkan Room, the Rumanian Suite, etc.' She shook her head resignedly. 'Those days have gone now, of course, and—well, there's really no more to tell . . .'

'Thank you, Miss Morrison, you've been very

helpful.' The Prince smiled at her. 'Perhaps you would be good enough to explain exactly what your position is, in this hotel?'

The effect of his smile hit her like a blow to the solar plexus, and for a moment she was breathless. 'My position . . .? Er . . . my position . . .' She attempted to collect herself. 'Well, none, officially. I would have liked to have had a proper training in hotel management, but,' she shrugged her shoulders helplessly, 'but it really hasn't been possible. There's so much to do just to keep the hotel running . . .'

Her voice trailed away as she suddenly realised she had nearly given away the true state of affairs at the Wivern Hotel. Sara closed her lips firmly. The Prince seemed to be having a peculiar effect on her, and she had no intention of giving him any further information. Really, this whole conversation was a complete waste of time! Pulling herself together, and avoiding his penetrating eyes, she said, 'Now, if you could please tell me exactly what's wrong, I . . .'

The Prince surprised her by rising from his chair. 'That, my dear Miss Morrison, would take more time than I have available at the moment. Please pay my respects to your father, and ask him to see me, when he has a moment. Thank you for calling.'

Sara's eyes flew to his face at his ironic tones. He knows! she thought despairingly. He knows all about this hotel. So why does he stay here? She was still trying to puzzle it out as she stood outside the suite, waiting for the lift to arrive. It was a conundrum she couldn't solve, as indeed had been her reaction to his commanding presence. However, as the lift arrived down in the foyer, and she was, as always, engulfed in the multifarious problems of a busy hotel, she forgot all about Prince Jabir.

Her father rolled in at six o'clock, very much the worse for wear, having had a good game of golf and a convivial time with his cronies, in the clubhouse.

'Oh God! You're in no state to be seen tonight,' Sara

regarded her father ruefully. She had long ago realised that it was a waste of time being angry with his neglect of the hotel, and his drinking. She turned despairingly to his companion. 'Can't you do *anything* with him?'

'Like what, darling?' drawled her father's girl-friend. Ann Harrington, dark, svelte and only a few years older than Sara, shrugged her shoulders. 'It's no use looking daggers at me, sweetie; he's always pleased himself and he's not going to stop now.'

Sara had no love for Ann, but she had to admit the justice of the dark girl's words. Clever, shrewd Ann— the merry divorcee! If she keeps on agreeing with his every thought and whim, she'll get him to the altar yet, Sara thought wryly.

A glance at her watch made her leap from her chair. 'Oh, hell! I forgot the cocktail party in the Balkan Room. I'll have a job to get ready in time. One of these nights I'll have a quiet evening off—if I get really lucky!'

She turned in the doorway. 'You'd better get Dad upstairs to the flat, Ann. Go the back way, we don't want anyone to see him like this,' and she hurried off to change.

Half an hour later she was greeting the President of the oil company in a long dress, whose simple lines clung to her figure, emphasising her small waist and full breasts. There had been no time to do anything with her long hair, except to brush it, and it hung in a golden stream down her back. The blue of the dress exactly matched her eyes, and she looked spectacularly beautiful. Certainly the President, Mr Milburn, thought so.

'Honey, you're a sight for sore eyes,' he enthused.

Sara laughed, and thanked him, before moving off to supervise the waiters. Mr Milburn, a widower, was an old and valued client, who liked her father or herself to be present at his parties, to make sure that all passed off smoothly.

The room started to fill up, and she was organising

the arrival of the hors d'oeuvres, when she looked up
and met Prince Jabir's eyes across the room. He was
staring intently at her, and Sara gave him a cool nod as
she proceeded with her duties as hostess. What's he
doing here? she thought crossly. Oil, of course—Arabs
and oil went together. Well, I've had quite enough of
him for one day!

An hour passed; the noise and the smoke increased in
volume as the oil men present settled down to their
familiar horse-trading, and their wives to Company
gossip. She tried not to look in Prince Jabir's direction,
but she was intently aware of his concentrated gaze.
Although he talked with the other guests, his eyes
seldom left her, as she moved through the room,
summoning a waiter to replenish an empty glass here,
or to take a tray of canapés there.

Sara found his presence and his obvious preoccupation with herself disturbing. He made her feel nervous
and selfconscious—for no good reason that she could
see, and as the party began to break up, she noticed out
of the corner of her eye that the Prince was moving
slowly but determinedly over to where she stood talking
to Mr Milburn.

Hurriedly she smiled at the President, and pleading a
headache, asked to be excused.

'Run along, honey. You've done us proud,' said Mr
Milburn, giving her a kiss on the cheek.

By the time she reached her room, she did indeed
have a headache. As she swallowed some aspirin, she
told herself it was the problems of the day which had
caused her head to throb so badly. It was nothing to do
with the Arab prince—nothing at all.

The next two weeks passed quietly, if everyday life
behind the scenes of a hotel could be called quiet. The
sauce chef gave in his notice, a new receptionist booked
two couples into the same room and one of the
chandeliers in the dining room fell down; fortunately
the latter happened in the morning, and not on the head
of an innocent diner. All par for the course, mused

Sara, as she tried to bring some order and method into the running of the hotel enterprise. An impossible task, she well knew, since her father gave her neither his support nor the financial responsibility which would have enabled her to carry out the job properly. If only he cared for the hotel, or was even interested in making it a viable concern. Maybe if her mother had lived . . .? Sara sighed, and turned once again to her perusal of the hotel accounts, which made depressing reading.

She woke up one morning in late May, and as the sun streamed in through her window, she realised that she had hardly been outside the hotel for the past fortnight. She would go for a walk in the park, she decided, and buy some summer clothes. The hotel could do without her for one day, at least. Jumping out of bed, and slipping into a dressing gown, she marched into the kitchen of the apartment, to find her father nursing his usual hangover.

'I'm going on strike today, Dad,' she told him firmly. 'I'm going out, and I won't be back till late. You, dearest father, can hold the fort for once.' Studiously ignoring his muffled protests, she dressed and left the hotel.

Intoxicated with the unexpected freedom, she returned pleasantly tired to the hotel in the early evening. She was surprised at the relief of the receptionist on duty. 'Thank God you've arrived, Sara!' she said. 'Your father's holding an impromptu party in the office, and I think it's getting out of hand.'

'Oh no!' groaned Sara in despair, as she hurriedly dropped her parcels behind the desk and ran to the office. She opened the door and stood rooted to the spot with amazement at the sight which met her eyes. Her father, champagne bottle in hand, was dancing on his desk, being clapped and applauded by his drinking cronies. She pushed her way through the throng, and with some difficulty attracted her father's attention.

'Who'sh my clever girlie, then,' he cried, as he

clambered off the desk and enveloped her in a hug.
'You've sh-saved our fortunes! Yesh, you have—Clever,
clever girlie!' He let her go suddenly, and she staggered
back as she watched with concern a drunken tear trickle
down his face. 'I'll miss you, you know. Yesh, I will,' he
shook his head at her as she tried to make some sort of
sense out of the situation.

'Miss me? Why will you miss me? What's going on?'
Sara queried, but she couldn't get a coherent answer
from her father, try as she might.

Spying Ann sitting in a corner, nursing a full
champagne glass, Sara forced her way through the
crowd. 'Maybe you can tell me what's going on, Ann.
This place is a madhouse, and what the hotel guests will
think . . .'

'Who cares!' replied Ann, with a peal of laughter.
'You're a dark horse, I must say!'

'Oh, for heaven's sake! Please, will someone tell me
what's happened?' Sara pleaded desperately.

'Your   father's   sold   the   hotel—that's   what's
happened, darling!' drawled Ann. 'And apparently it's
all your doing.'

'*Sold the hotel? My doing?* you're all out of your
minds!'

'It's true, sweetie. Your dear old dad has sold the
hotel to that Arab prince—something or other—and
apparently you're going to marry him—the Prince, I
mean.' Ann hiccuped, and took another sip from her
glass.

'*I'm what!*' Sara stood gazing at Ann in horror. She
eventually pulled herself together, and gave a shaky
laugh. 'Come on, Ann—a joke's a joke. Tell me what's
really happened?'

'Darling, I ash-assure you it's true. Really! The Arab
that's staying in the Rumanian Suite—you know the
one—well, he called your father in to see him this
morning, and the solicitors this afternoon. Well, bar the
shouting, he's bought the hotel, for at least twice what
it's worth! Your dear old dad can't believe his luck.'

'Well . . .' said Sara slowly, 'I'm glad for Dad, of course, but . . .' She suddenly remembered the rest of Ann's words. 'What's all this nonsense about my marrying Prince Jabir?'

'Darling, I wasn't there, but your father says that the Prince asked for your hand in marriage—too sweet in this day and age—and your father gave his blessing.'

'Oh, did he? Did he indeed!' Sara couldn't remember when she had last felt so angry. 'Well, he can just take his "blessing" back! I'm certainly *not* going to marry the Prince. The whole thing is absolutely ridiculous!'

'Oh yes,' said Ann solemnly, the amount of champagne she had consumed catching up with her rapidly. 'No marriage—no sale. That's what the Prince said.'

'We'll see about *that*!' retorted Sara, as she pushed her way through the drunken crowd to the office door. She stormed across the foyer and into the lift, her temper rising with each floor she passed. As the Arab servant opened the door at her perfunctory knock, she brushed him aside, as she marched into the Prince's lounge.

'Just what's going on?' she demanded furiously of Prince Jabir, who was sitting reading in one of the easy chairs.

He looked up and regarded the girl as she stood in front of him, trembling with rage. 'You seem angry, Miss Morrison,' he said in a firm voice, devoid of any expression.

'Angry? I'm not just angry—I'm livid! I've just been told by my father's . . . my father's girl-friend that he's sold the hotel to you, and . . . and . . .' She couldn't bring herself to say the rest of the words. Maybe Ann had been playing a trick? In this quiet room, the whole idea that the Prince would want to marry her seemed impossible. It must be a mistake. *It must!*

'You are quite right, I have indeed bought the hotel from your father. I am sure it will prove to be an excellent investment—properly run, of course.' He paused, and looked at Sara, still standing, trembling in front of him. 'Please sit down, Sara, and calm down as well. All this shouting and fury achieves nothing.'

Sara suddenly felt very tired, and emotionally exhausted. 'I'm sorry,' she said as she settled into a chair opposite him. 'It's—it's just been a shock. I've never known any home other than the hotel. I . . .'

'I realise that,' said the Prince. 'Now, we will have some coffee and talk,' and he clapped his hands. The sound brought the servant into the room immediately. Prince Jabir gave an order in Arabic and a few minutes later Sara was drinking some of the best coffee she had ever tasted.

'Hamid is a genius at making coffee—I don't know what I'd do without him. Now,' Prince Jabir continued, 'all this furious rage of yours—it cannot just be the sale of the hotel. I am therefore assuming that your father's . . . er . . . girl-friend will no doubt have told you of my offer of marriage.'

'*So it's true!*' whispered Sara, gazing at him with horrified eyes. 'You must be mad!'

'Not at all,' the Prince said calmly. 'In my country it is customary to consult the father before speaking to the woman.'

'But why?' wailed Sara, so confused that she could hardly think straight. 'Why on earth do you want to marry me?'

'I have some very good reasons, which we will go into later. However,' he continued, in the same maddeningly calm voice, 'let us look, logically, at why you should marry me. For too long, I suspect, you have been a drudge in this hotel. Your father clearly has no interest in its running, and you have been the general dogsbody, at everyone's beck and call. Yes?'

Sara nodded dumbly, as he went on. 'So, the hotel is sold, and your father is comfortable. He can afford to indulge himself. Maybe buy a house and, possibly, marry his . . . er . . . lady-friend.' He paused, looking at the dejected girl before him, as the truth of his words struck home.

'What will happen to you, do you think? Would you be happy with such a stepmother? Would she make you welcome at your father's house? You are young, and . . .'

'I'm twenty,' mumbled Sara, still in shock, 'and—and I can look after myself.'

'Assuredly,' the calm voice continued inexorably. 'Your life stretches in front of you—but what are you trained for? Let us see: You can run a hotel, but alas you have no paper qualifications. You are a good hostess and, I must further add, you are very beautiful.'

Sara raised her head to look at Prince Jabir, and finding his gaze as disturbing as ever, she looked quickly down at her hands clasped tightly in her lap, as a blush spread over her cheeks.

'So, we have this beautiful girl, who can run a large establishment, and act as a good hostess—and there you have in a nutshell why it is that I wish to marry you. I have a need for a wife who possesses just your qualities—and I offer you a contract for our mutual benefit.'

'A—a *contract*? I . . . I don't understand.' Sara closed her eyes weakly, as her stunned mind strove to comprehend all he was saying.

'The problem is, in essence, a simple one. My father, King Abdul al Shakir, is the ruler of the Kingdom of Assir, which protrudes like a finger into the Arabian Gulf. It was a small, poor desert state, of no particular importance, until the late 1950s. Then oil was discovered, and like many of the other desert countries we fell heir to problems that are exactly the opposite to those you have here, in the West. Put simply—we have *too* much money.

'We have, of course, built hospitals and schools, and brought my country forward into the twentieth century. However, the oil revenues continue to pour in.' The Prince looked over at Sara. 'Do you follow me, so far?'

'Yes, of course.' Sara brushed a tired and nervous hand across her forehead. 'But I don't see . . .'

'Just listen,' interjected the Prince, 'and all will become clear. My father is an infinitely wise man, and he foresaw the problems that were likely to rise. He therefore had me educated here in England, and at the Harvard Business School. For the past six years I have been in charge of investing our surplus oil revenue, both in Europe and America. It means that I have to spend much of the year travelling in the West, arranging business contracts and making investment decisions.' He broke off, to order more coffee, and then continued.

'As a result of the business in which I am engaged, I find that I have to do a considerable amount of entertaining, often at short notice—and I have the need for a decorative wife who will handle that side of my life. I also,' he added, 'would expect you to be a mother to my two little girls, Nadia aged seven and Mara aged five. I would like to see more of them than I do at present.'

'A mother?' Sara felt a rising tide of hysteria, and strove to explain, 'I can't . . . I mean, it's so impossible. Surely their mother . . .?'

The prince's face became masklike and stern, as he rasped, 'My wife . . .' he hesitated, 'my wife is dead.'

Sara felt a wave of sympathy. 'I'm so sorry, Prince . . . er . . . Jabir.'

He raised his hand, and Sara fell silent. It seemed he did not welcome or want her sympathy.

'Please call me by my given name,' he said, 'this "prince" business is unnecessary between us, Sara.' He looked directly at her, as he continued, 'I need a wife, a Western wife, to solve the domestic and business problems that I have outlined to you. In return you would live, as they say, in the lap of luxury. Your father will be provided for, and you could bring much happiness and pleasure to my children.'

'But—but, Prince . . . I mean, Jabir . . .' It was all too much for Sara, who gestured helplessly. 'You don't understand! You know nothing about me ... and it's quite impossible, this whole crazy idea of yours. I ... I mean, I don't love you ...'

'My dear Sara, what do you think I've been doing for the last two weeks? I have your complete dossier on that table over there. I imagine I know more about you than you do yourself!'

'What you mean you ... *How dare you* ...!' Almost choking with rage, Sara glared at him.

'Have some sense, Sara. I would be a very poor businessman if I brought a company without investigating its background, wouldn't I? As to the "love" you speak of; of course you don't love me, and neither do I love you. It is a completely unnecessary preoccupation of the Western mind. I am talking about a contract—a partnership.'

'In other words ...' Sara was breathless with outrage, 'in other words you're intending to *buy* me! I've never heard anything so archaic—never in my whole life!' She jumped to her feet. 'I've heard quite enough of this nonsense. Believe me, there's no way I would ever ...'

Jabir had also risen, his firm cool hand grasped her wrist in a vice-like grip, his close proximity setting tremors fluttering in her stomach.

'Come, you are tired. It has been a long day. Go and think over my proposition, and talk to your future stepmother.' He smiled at her. 'I consider her likely to be my best advocate.'

'There is nothing—absolutely *nothing*—that would induce me to marry you, Jabir. You can forget this whole stupid idea, immediately!' Sara snatched her hand away, and strode off to the door. Struck by a sudden thought, she turned to face him. 'Ann said ...' she hesitated a moment. 'Ann said that ... that you wouldn't buy the hotel, if ... if I don't agree to marry you.'

Jabir nodded. 'Quite correct.'

'But why? I don't understand. I ...'

Jabir shrugged. 'Because I need to settle my domestic

affairs more than I need a hotel, of course.' He turned back to his chair. 'Go and rest, Sara. I am flying to Paris tomorrow. I will be back for your answer in two days' time.'

Sara, speechless with fury, couldn't think of anything rude enough with which to express her feelings, and contented herself with slamming the door loudly behind her.

As she lay in bed that night, the conversation with Jabir kept going around and around her head. She was quite intelligent enough to see the cards stacked against her refusal of his mad proposition. Ann and her father would undoubtedly bring mounting pressure to bear upon her. *I won't be bought!* was her last despairing thought as she lapsed into the welcome arms of sleep.

'*Madame,* please fasten your seatbelt, we are about to descend.'

The stewardess's voice dragged Sara back to the present. Her fingers fumbled with the belt, as she saw her husband rise from his desk and walk back towards the seat beside her. His tall, broad-shouldered figure seemed to fill the cabin, and not for the first time that day she felt lonely, frightened and afraid of the unknown life before her.

CHAPTER TWO

THE warmth of Nice Airport was a welcome change from the cool, rainy London they had left behind. Sara stood on the tarmac by the aeroplane, talking idly to her husband's assistant, John Morgan, as their luggage was removed from the private jet. A large black Cadillac drew up, and the chauffeur, an Arab, jumped out and opened a door for her.

Sara turned apprehensive eyes on John Morgan. 'Where are we going now?'

'Just over there to the helicopter.' He pointed across the airfield. 'It's only a short hop to the yacht—it doesn't take long to get to Cannes.' His warm American voice, and his frank admiration, cheered her. 'If you'll just go with Youssef the chauffeur,' he continued, 'I and the Prince will join you in a few minutes, when we've dealt with the French Customs officials.'

She looked at the mound of luggage. 'I suppose we are going to be able to get all that into the helicopter? It looks a lot.'

'It should be O.K., but Youssef can take anything that won't fit in back to the yacht.'

Sara was flabbergasted. 'You mean . . . you mean he drove all the way here, just to take us across from the aeroplane to the helicopter? I—I don't believe it!' Was this how the super-rich lived? She blinked in bewilderment.

'He sure did. It's much quicker by air,' answered John, 'and the Prince sets a fast pace.'

Youssef helped her up the steps into the white helicopter, before returning for the rest of the party. Sara looked around her with interest. The interior, although functional, contained six seats, and she chose one at the back, while she waited for the others to join her. Surely there ought to be someone here to fly this machine, she wondered idly, as Jabir, John and Hamid, Jabir's servant, climbed aboard.

Her question was answered as she saw Jabir settle into the pilot's seat, clamp on the earphones, and start the rotor blades. He turned to make sure that all their safety-belts were fastened, and as his blank, impersonal gaze swept past her, Sara shivered at the thought of the loveless marriage which lay before her.

The helicopter lifted off the tarmac, and soon they were on their way, out over the blue Mediterranean Sea, following the coast. The chugging of the rotor blades had a soothing effect on Sara. She watched Jabir at the controls, as his strong hands moved over the dials, and he bent his powerful concentration to the job in hand. Just remember he's ruthless, she told herself. Big, dark and completely ruthless! Certainly the pressures he had applied to gain her agreement to their 'marriage' had been formidable.

She had woken the morning after her talk with Jabir, feeling like death warmed up, and had gone to the kitchen to make a comforting cup of tea. It was with heavy eyes and a sense of impending doom that she watched Ann enter the kitchen.

She can certainly hold her drink, thought Sara gloomily, as Ann cheerfully bade her 'Good morning' and put on the kettle for her usual cup of coffee.

'There's nothing good about this morning,' said Sara grimly. 'In fact it looks like being a perfectly dreadful day—especially if your cheerful face is anything to go by!'

Ann didn't reply, and continued making her coffee, before coming over to sit down at the kitchen table. 'Look, Sara, let's cut out the wisecracks, shall we? You can be as rude to me as you like—I probably would act the same way if I were in your shoes. However, it's not very constructive behaviour at the best of times, and certainly not now.'

Ann looked searchingly at the dejected girl in front of

her. 'I take it that the idea of marrying Prince Jabir doesn't appeal to you?'

'No, it certainly doesn't!'

'Why not?' probed Ann. 'He's devastatingly handsome, and as rich as Croesus.'

'I don't care how good-looking or wealthy he is,' wailed Sara. 'He doesn't want to marry me for any of the usual reasons—in fact he doesn't want to marry *me* at all. He's trying to buy me, like . . . like he'd buy a new company, and he's only interested in getting a good return for his . . . his investment!' and she burst into a storm of tears.

Ann was surprisingly kind and gentle, as she helped Sara to dry her eyes, and then made her a fresh cup of tea. Replenishing her own coffee cup, she sat down at the table once more.

'Let's forget the Prince for the moment, Sara, and look at your future here in this place, if matters go on as they have done for the past few years.' Ann paused to sip her coffee, and continued, 'Your father doesn't really give a damn what happens to the hotel. He's simply not cut out to be a hotelier—and it's a great pity he didn't have any brothers or sisters who might have made a go of it instead.'

Sara looked up in surprise. This wasn't the usual Ann speaking.

'There's no need to look so amazed,' said Ann, correctly interpreting Sara's expression. 'I'm quite happy to act the "poor little me" for your father's benefit, if that's what he wants.' She looked Sara straight in the eye. 'I really do love him, you know. Which doesn't mean that I'm blind to all his faults, because I'm not. I fully intend to marry him,' she continued, 'and we'll settle down in a nice house by a golf course, and live a thoroughly boring life. Believe me, he'll be very happy.

'However, before that happens, both you and I know that this hotel will slide further and further into the red, despite all your valiant efforts. The bank will then foreclose, and there'll be a lot of jolly creditors' meetings all around!'

'It's surely not as bad as all that . . .' Sara responded defensively.

'Oh yes, it is, and well you know it. Come on, Sara! Stop fooling yourself. This place is on a one-way ticket to disaster, and unless someone like the Prince comes along soon . . .' she snapped her fingers, 'it's strictly "finito" for all of us.'

Reluctantly, Sara had to agree that Ann was right. For a long time now she had refused to accept the stark truth. It suddenly all seemed such a waste . . .

'Mind you,' Ann's voice interrupted her thoughts, 'properly run, it could be a little goldmine, but it needs so much money spent on it first. Well, you must know the problems better than I do.'

Sara nodded slowly, and gave a deep sigh. 'You're right, of course. Still . . .'

'Oh, Sara, let's face it—that damned Arab has got us all by the whatsits! Make no mistake, he's blackmailing us all—not just you. He *knows* that I'm going to have to put pressure on you. I'm going to have to force you to face the grim, economic reality of the hotel's future. Not to mention, I may add, that he must have a very good idea that I don't exactly relish the thought of such a good-looking stepdaughter. No woman, however saintly, wants that sort of competition . . . certainly not this close to home!'

'He said you would be his best advocate,' muttered Sara unhappily.

'There you are! He really is a clever devil. If we weren't all so involved, I'd admire his finesse. I bet he's a real killer shark in the business world. As it is, I have an overwhelming urge to strangle his handsome neck! The only person who's completely oblivious to all this, of course, is your father,' added Ann. 'He's in such a happy haze at the prospect of an escape from a life he hates that the cruel light of day is unlikely to get a look in. Don't go to him for any help, because I'm afraid you won't get it.'

Sara felt depression settling on her like a heavy blanket. 'Yes, we all know Dad. Ann, can't you help? What can I do?' she cried.

'With the best will in the world—and being as honest as I can—I don't see that you have a choice. There is an alternative, of course. If maybe you were a different person, tougher, more like me—then you'd be able to consign us all to hell! You'd be able to walk out of the hotel without a backward glance, and start a new life on your own. But you won't be able to do that, will you? I don't think you're capable of standing by, letting the hotel go broke, and watching your father's world crashing about his ears. And since you can't do that . . .'

'. . . . I don't have any alternative but to accept the Prince's *contract*, do I?' Sunk in the deepest gloom, Sara finished the sentence.

'Frankly, no.' Ann hesitated, then spoke bracingly. 'What I think you've got to do is to start thinking positively about it all. He told your father about his young children. Surely if you concentrated on them . . .? Apparently their mother is dead, and they don't see their father very much. Well, if you tried to make them happy, that would at least be something you could do.'

Despite her predicament, Sara couldn't help laughing. 'That's rich, coming from you! I never imagined that the patter of tiny feet would be exactly your thing.'

'No,' Ann grinned back at her, 'but I think it may well be yours. You've got a well-developed sense of responsibility, possibly over-developed. Just look at the way you've slaved in this hotel—and for precious little thanks. Yes . . .' she regarded Sara speculatively, 'I think you'd make a very good stepmother, and that certainly is more than you could say for me.'

'Oh, Ann! You've been so kind. I'm . . . I'm so sorry we haven't been friends before now.'

'Drama brings out the best in me, didn't you know?' Ann smiled wryly. 'It wouldn't have worked—the three of us in this hotel. You won't believe me now, but I think, in the end, you may find that you're very happy. No one likes to be forced into anything—and that's what you resent, isn't it?' She stood up, and stretched lazily. 'Come on, it's time we got dressed. Why don't you go and have a shower, it might make you feel better. You never know—you might come up with a brilliant solution to your problem.'

During the next two days Sara did indeed try to solve the dilemma in which she found herself. She tried to talk to her father, although she knew in her heart that it was a waste of time. He just smiled at her, until she had finished what she was saying, then gave her a big kiss.

'You'll have a wonderful life, darling. You're just suffering from pre-wedding nerves,' he said, patting her kindly on the back. 'Everything will be fine—just you see.'

During the remainder of that day, and the sleepless night that followed, Sara wrestled with the problem, but to no avail. Ann was right, she couldn't just walk out and leave her father to cope—even if it was a mess of his own making. She was, therefore, mentally and physically exhausted by the time she found herself once again in the Rumanian Suite, reluctantly agreeing to marry Prince Jabir.

'So, we have a contract, Sara.' His hooded eyes looked at her searchingly for a moment, then he said, 'Whatever your feelings, I believe you will undertake to meet my conditions as honestly as you can—yes?'

'Yes,' she whispered in agreement, staring down at her clenched hands.

His normally impassive face softened for a moment, as he viewed the figure hunched miserably in front of him. 'Come, Sara, it won't be such a bad life, you know; and do I really strike you as such a terrible monster?'

'Oh no!' Sara raised her eyes, full of unshed tears, to his face. 'Oh, no—I didn't mean . . .'

'It's just not how you planned you life?'

'Yes,' she agreed quickly. How could she possibly

explain to this man what she had not been able to say even to Ann; that it was the disturbing effect he had on her that was exacerbating the problem. Whenever he was near, she felt flustered and nervous. The hotel and her father—however troublesome—were known factors. With them, she felt safe. She didn't feel at all safe with Jabir, quite the reverse, and she didn't understand it at all.

'Very well,' said Jabir. 'We must now make some plans quickly, as I leave for New York tomorrow. I suggest we marry when I get back, in two weeks' time.'

He had called in John Morgan, and given his assistant the task of arranging the details, such as the special licence, register office and the hotel wedding reception. When John left the room, Jabir moved over to sit beside Sara on the sofa.

'Give me your hand,' he said, removing a small box from his pocket.

Mystified, she did as she was told, her eyes widening as he slipped a huge diamond ring on her finger. 'Oh, Jabir!' she exclaimed, confused. 'It isn't necessary—I never thought . . .'

'Nonsense, we must do the thing properly—and seal our contract.' Raising his hand, he ran a finger gently down the side of her face and tilted her chin up towards him.

She was totally unprepared for his kiss, and she gasped as his firm, warm mouth possessed her own lips. As quickly as his mouth had descended, it was withdrawn, and he stood up and went over to a table at the end of the room.

'Champagne, Sara? As a good Moslem, I don't usually drink, but we must try to inject some *joie de vivre* into this situation, don't you think?'

Breathless and lightheaded, Sara could only nod dumbly. Her heart was thudding and she felt most peculiar. The champagne helped to clear her head, however, and she began to feel slightly calmer.

'Go to Harrods for your trousseau,' said Jabir. 'I

have an account there, so get anything you may need. John will be able to give you a list of my future engagements, which will give you some idea of the clothes you will require.' He paused for thought, and said, 'I think I've covered everything—is there anything you'd like to ask me?'

Sara cleared her throat nervously. 'Yes—what happens if . . . I mean . . . things may not work out. Your children . . . they might not like me, or . . .'

'I certainly would not try to keep you against your will. If you were really unhappy—for whatever reason—you would be free to go. Divorce is very easy for a Moslem, you know.' His voice suddenly sounded very harsh, and she looked up in surprise.

He collected himself, and continued in an even tone, 'However, I am expecting you to honour our contract, to the best of your ability.' He watched the varying expressions flit across her face. 'The answers to your next two questions are: No, you do not have to take my faith, unless you decide you wish to; and Yes, you would be my only wife.'

'How did you know . . .' she blushed.

'My dear Sara, your face is very expressive!' He smiled. 'I have no difficulty in reading your thoughts, good or bad. Now to other matters. I will be away until our wedding. If you need any assistance, John will be here. Don't hesitate to call on his services.'

Sara moved like a sleepwalker through the following two weeks, her only small consolation having been her new-found friendship with Ann, who had proved to be a staunch supporter. She protected Sara from much of her father's euphoria at her marriage and the sale of his hotel.

She had woken this morning—was it really *this morning*, it already seemed light years away—to find the weather outside a drizzle, exactly matching her mood.

Moving like an automaton through the marriage ceremony, she stood in a haze of unreality as the reception eddied and flowed around her numb figure, until Jabir touched her arm.

'Ten more minutes, and then we must go.'

Her brief farewells were soon over. She was standing outside the hotel shivering with nervous exhaustion, as much as from the unexpectedly cold weather, when Jabir clicked his fingers. Hamid came forward to hand him a pale cream-coloured mink coat, which he placed around her shoulders.

'Just a small wedding present,' he said dismissively, as she regarded both him and the soft fur with incredulity. 'You must take care not to catch cold,' he added, taking no notice of her stuttered thanks, as he directed her into a chauffeured limousine for the drive to Heathrow Airport.

Sara was jolted from her thoughts by a tapping on her shoulder. She turned, to see John pointing downwards. Looking out of the window, she saw below a large ship riding at anchor in the bay. It looks more like the *Queen Elizabeth* than a yacht! she thought incredulously.

The helicopter slowly descended and landed gently on the top deck of the vessel. Leaving Jabir to complete the landing checks, John escorted her out and took her down in a lift to the main part of the yacht, which seemed to consist of one pile-carpeted stateroom after another.

'Would you like a drink, Princess?' queried John.

'Yes, please! That would be marvellous, it's—it's been quite a day.' Sara sank down on one of the soft chairs, feeling tired to death. 'Please call me Sara,' she added.

'Nope, I'm afraid I can't do that,' he smiled ruefully at her. 'The Prince really wouldn't like it. He's a very formal kind of guy, you know.'

'Yes, I know,' she sighed, and sipped her whisky. She was just wondering whether anything ever ruffled her new husband's bland exterior, when Jabir arrived in the room.

'Ah, I see John has been looking after you.' He turned to his assistant. 'Please show my wife to her room. I expect she is tired and would like to rest before dinner. I'm going to the office, I'll see you there in a few minutes,' and he left without giving Sara another glance.

A spark of anger flamed within her. How dared he talk about her as if she was just a piece of furniture to be moved around? But, too weary to bother about anything more that day, she trailed down a wide corridor behind John.

Moments later she found herself in a large bedroom, being introduced to a French girl. 'Marie is your maid on the yacht, and when you travel in the West,' said John, turning to leave. 'You'll have other servants in Assir, of course.'

'Of course,' she echoed dully. 'I—I think I'll just lie down for a bit,' she said to the girl. She'd never had a personal maid before; what was one supposed to do with them?'

'Certainement, madame.' Marie proved immensely helpful, helping her to undo her zip, and hanging her dress in a capacious wardrobe, before she too vanished and Sara was alone. Waves of fatigue overwhelmed her, and quite unable to take in her luxurious surroundings, she crawled into bed and fell fast asleep.

She was awakened by a hand touching her shoulder, and opened her eyes to find Jabir sitting beside her on the bed. She looked sleepily around the room. It must be late, she thought as she noticed that the curtains were drawn, the bedroom being lit by soft lamps. Still semi-drugged from her deep sleep, she looked at Jabir, dressed in a pale blue towelling robe, which accentuated his creamy skin and black hair. Ann was right, she thought dreamily, he *is* sensationally attractive!

As she lay on the pillows looking up at him, his hand moved to toy with the tendrils of her long blonde hair, which lay fanned about her head. 'You are looking very beautiful, Sara,' he said slowly, as his fingers moved to stroke her shoulder. His touch on her bare flesh started nervous tremors fluttering through her body, and her heart began to beat rapidly as she saw the gleam in his dark eyes.

'No ... please, no ...' she whispered as he gently slid the thin strap of her petticoat down off her shoulder. Her startled cry as his hand moved to explore her exposed breast was smothered by his descending mouth, warm and firm, which possessed her in a determined fashion, without passion or tenderness. She tried to struggle, but her puny efforts had no effect, as his mouth moved calmly and deliberately over her lips, forcing them apart, and moulding them to his will.

Sara felt as though she was drowning, swamped by feelings she didn't know existed, and which she had never experienced before. Aeons of time seemed to pass before he withdrew his lips and looked down at her, as she lay stunned and breathless, his hands moving gently over her taut breasts.

She slowly opened her fluttering eyelids, and blushed a deep crimson, as Jabir took his hands from her body and rose to walk over to the window. She was scrambling for a sheet to cover herself, as he turned and looked at her.

'It is important that I know—for your own sake, Sara—whether you are a virgin.'

'*What!* Of course I ...' she said, floundering, as she regarded him with angry embarrassment. 'You have no *right* to ...' She gasped, and blushed again, as she looked at him in dawning horror.

Jabir shrugged his shoulders. 'Who can tell nowadays? The behaviour of modern youth is inexplicable.' He moved, and immediately her stomach knotted with tension. But he merely walked over to sit down in an armchair by the bed. He bent his concentrated gaze on the frightened and dishevelled girl on the bed, and his lips twitched in a sardonic grin.

'Oh Sara, Sara! There was *one subject* we didn't discuss, wasn't there?' He gave a bark of dry laughter. 'Don't tell me that it had never occurred to you?' There was a pause while he studied her intently, and then he laughed again.

'I can see that it didn't. Virginal in mind as well as body! My dear girl, it's a perfectly normal bodily function between consenting adults—especially when they are married. Making love is not something to be frightened of.'

'That's the most—the most cold-blooded thing I've ever heard!' Sara wailed. 'It's not . . . it's not my idea of m-m-making love!' and she turned to bury her face in the pillows. A moment later she raised her head, her eyes brimming with tears. 'And I'm not *consenting* either. That wasn't . . . it wasn't in the contract . . . you've just said so!' She glared at him defiantly.

'Ah!' There was a long pause, before Jabir stood up. 'Well, I have never raped anyone, and I'm certainly not proposing to start now. I suggest that we leave this whole distressing subject alone for the time being.' He turned and opened a door which clearly connected his room with hers. 'I think you should ring for your maid—dinner will be ready in an hour.' He left, the door clicking silently behind him.

Left alone, Sara gave way to some tears, before getting out of bed and opening her overnight case. She removed and slipped into a wrap, before exploring the room in search of the bell, which soon brought Marie.

'I—I'd like a bath, please,' she said, 'but I don't know where the bathroom is.'

'*Voilà, madame,*' gestured Marie, opening yet another door to display a capacious modern bathroom, covered in pink marble throughout.

Lying in the soothing warmth of the scented water, Sara considered her position. It was no good giving way to self-pity, she told herself ruefully, as tears started to flow again. She had accepted this marriage with her

eyes open, and it was hardly Jabir's fault if she hadn't
considered the full implications of what it involved. She
had fought against being trapped into a loveless
marriage—a contract—but it was no good blaming him
for the loss of her romantic illusions.

To love, and be loved. That was surely what any girl
of her age had a right to expect from marriage? Jabir
had made his position clear from the start—he had
laughed at the idea of love and all it stood for. His idea
of marriage was a 'business' partnership. It wasn't
surprising that she hadn't considered the physical side
of marriage with Jabir. He had been so busy laying
down conditions and terms. How could she have
guessed that . . . Sara flushed with mortification at her
own stupidity.

A nervous shiver ran through her as she remembered
Jabir's kiss. It wouldn't be so bad if she was indifferent
to him, but he had the ability to make her feel so . . . so
like a quick dose of 'flu, she thought. She shook her
head in bafflement at feelings and sensations she didn't
understand, and stepped out of the bath.

As she towelled herself dry, she tried to calm her
nerves and consider the position dispassionately. Jabir
had, after all, kept his side of the bargain—very
generously, she had to admit. If need be, she supposed,
it was up to her to honour hers. Although how she
could face the experience, with someone who called
making love a 'natural bodily function', and who didn't
love or even particularly care for her . . .? She had to
grit her teeth to stop herself from giving way to tears
again.

She was sitting in front of the mirror, while Marie
brushed her long hair, when Jabir re-entered the
room. He was wearing a white dinner jacket, which
contrasted sharply with his dark good looks. His broad
shoulders filled the doorway, and his commanding
presence dominated the room. He looks fabulous, she
thought, as her heart started beating nervously once
again.

Marie had unpacked and put away most of her clothes, and had gently urged Sara to choose a gold dress, the same shade as her hair. She had been doubtful, but Marie had been certain. *'C'est parfait, madame.'*

Jabir snapped his fingers dismissively, and Marie put down the brush, bobbed a curtsy, and left the room. Sara sat, a still golden statue, holding her breath as he moved to stand behind her, their eyes locking together in the mirror.

'At—or should I say, despite—the risk of being accused of bribery, let alone corruption,' he said in a dry voice, 'I think that this will become you,' and he reached forward to place a necklace around her throat.

She swept her hair aside to enable him to fit the clasp, and gasped as the full magnificence of his gift met her eyes. A choker of diamonds encircled her throat, emphasising her slender neck and the swell of her breasts in the low-cut dress. Her hands flew to the necklace in wonder. 'I—I don't know what to say! I've never ... I can't ...'

'There is no need to say anything. Come, dinner is waiting,' and he took her arm to help her rise from the dressing stool.

'Please——' Sara placed a restraining hand on his sleeve. 'I'm sorry I was so stupid, earlier. You were quite right, I hadn't ... hadn't considered ...' she swallowed nervously. 'I'm truly very grateful for all your gifts, I really am. I ...'

Jabir smiled down at her anxious face. 'We can discuss it all later. Far more important, I'm ashamed to say, is the fact that I'm starving! Come along.'

As they walked to the dining room, she noticed for the first time a humming sound, and felt the yacht move slightly. She turned her head to look at Jabir, and he confirmed her thoughts. 'Yes, we have just started for the open sea. We will have a few days cruising around the Mediterranean, and then return to Cannes.'

The dining room was magnificent, and the dinner was

delicious, but Sara found herself looking at her helping of strawberries and cream with mounting distaste. The shrimp cocktail had been fine, but it had proved an increasing struggle to force down the spring lamb, and now . . . beads of perspiration broke out on her forehead as her stomach lurched and turned over.

She stood up, swaying slightly. 'I'm so sorry, but . . . but I feel very ill . . .' and she rushed from the room.

Thank God she had reached the bathroom in time, she consoled herself, as she rested her fevered head on the cool marble wall. She felt another rising tide of nausea—and she was sick again. Marie hurried in, much concerned, *'Oh, mon Dieu! C'est mal de mer,'* she clucked, as she helped Sara out of the lovely gold dress.

Half an hour later, when the worst seemed to be over, Marie slipped a nightdress on her and helped her into bed, where she collapsed with a groan.

Some time during the night she felt a cool compress being placed on her forehead. Half awake, she gazed up, as Jabir's face swam in front of her feverish eyes.

'I'm dying,' she moaned.

'No, my dear wife, you're not dying. You are just being seasick, which is *another thing* that didn't occur to either of us!'

He continued to gently swab her forehead, as she groaned and lapsed, once more, into an unconscious void.

CHAPTER THREE

Two days passed before Sara, looking at the sunlight streaming through the large square windows of her bedroom on the yacht, realised that she might be going to live after all. Never in all her life had she felt so ill. Leaning weakly against the soft pillows, she thought again of how kind and considerate Jabir had been. Every time she had surfaced from the depths of her sickness, he had been there with cold flannels and kind words of encouragement.

There was a knock at the door and her husband entered, followed by Marie bearing a tray.

'Good morning, Sara. I hear that you are feeling much better. I also hear that you have refused to have anything to eat,' he added in a stern voice.

Sara looked reproachfully at Marie, who shrugged, pulling a face at Jabir's back.

'Your maid put up a valiant smokescreen on your behalf, but it was important for your health's sake that I found out the truth,' said Jabir, who seemed to have eyes in the back of his head.

His tall and immaculate, if casually dressed figure, dominated the room. Sara, very conscious of the semi-nudity of her thin silk nightgown, blushed and struggled to sit up, while at the same time trying to keep herself covered by the bedclothes.

'I'm sorry, Jabir, but the thought of food—any food—is just . . .' She looked on helplessly as, taking no notice of her protests, he gestured to Marie to place a tray on her lap. The maid gave her a small smile of sympathy and then hurriedly bobbed a curtsy and left the room at a snap of Jabir's fingers.

Drawing up a chair to her bedside, he sat down and calmly began to pour her a cup of tea.

'Tea and dry toast are hardly "food", Sara. Come along, eat and drink up,' he commanded.

She tried to repress a shudder. 'I—I can't . . .' she said weakly. 'I'm sorry to have been such a nuisance, but . . .'

'Drink your tea,' said Jabir in a steely tone.

She hesitated, but a swift glance at his hard, firm and determined features persuaded her that she had no choice but to obey. As she sipped the hot liquid, she thought again how unexpectedly kind Jabir had been.

'I'm really very sorry about—about being so seasick. I feel such a fool! I'm so grateful for all you did for me, I really am.'

'Then you will gratify me by eating your toast,' Jabir said firmly. As she hesitated, he smiled, 'Come on, Sara, it will do you good.'

Helplessly bemused by his unexpected smile, which made her feel suddenly breathless, she began to nibble a piece of toast.

'That's better. You should be all right now that the yacht has docked. We must just make sure we do not risk taking you on the open sea again.'

'Docked?' she looked puzzled. 'You mean we aren't moving?'

Jabir laughed. 'Oh, Sara, it is plain you will never be a sailor! My dear wife, as soon as you became sick it was clear we must make for land immediately. The yacht has been stationary for some time.'

'Where are we? Back in Cannes?'

'Certainly not!' He gave her a sardonic grin. 'Cannes is hardly my idea of a quiet honeymoon. As to where we are—you must come up on deck and see for yourself.'

'I'm not sure I . . . er . . . feel quite well enough.' Jabir's use of the words 'wife' and 'honeymoon' had forcibly reminded her of the facts of her situation. She began to colour faintly as she looked at his hard firm mouth, and the dark hooded eyes set over his high cheekbones.

Nervously clutching the sheet closer, she tried to ignore a rising tide of panic. 'I—I think I'll just stay in bed for a bit, if you don't mind.'

'But I do mind, Sara,' said Jabir, with a faint smile, accompanied by a disturbing glint in his eyes. 'It will be good for you to have some fresh air,' he added firmly, as he rose to take her tray. 'See, you have eaten all your toast, and now feel much better, yes?'

'No, I don't,' she muttered crossly, and threw him a glance of dislike, as he ignored her and walked towards the door.

'Have a shower and get dressed,' he commanded inexorably. 'I will be back in half an hour. If you are not ready, I will just have to dress you myself.'

'Stop bullying me!' she protested, glaring balefully at his departing figure. Jabir's only reply was a bark of dry laughter, as the door closed behind him.

There was no doubt in Sara's mind that Jabir meant every word he had said, and was quite capable of putting his threat into action. Her thoughts strayed back to her wedding night. She remembered his warm possessive mouth, his firm hands on her body ... Blushing furiously at the recollection, she quickly rang the bell for Marie, and with her assistance staggered on weak legs into the bathroom. Surveying herself in the mirror, she was taken aback to see how pale and wan she looked.

Even later, as she tried to disguise with make-up the dark shadows beneath her brilliant blue eyes, she felt depressed. You look awful, she told herself gloomily, really awful. Just like death warmed up. Heaven knows what Jabir will think! Serve him right for being such a bully, she thought mulishly, and then immediately felt contrite. It couldn't have been much fun for him, having to look after a sick wife, and alter all his plans for a Mediterranean cruise. He could, after all, have left her to Marie, and not bothered at all. In fact, considering how he seemed to treat those around him, snapping his fingers at his servants, for instance, his care and kindness for her comfort seemed totally out of character! The trouble was, she thought as she surveyed her pale face, it was very difficult to understand a man who seemed to be more inscrutable than the Sphinx.

It was, as usual, impossible to guess what her husband thought as he stood in the doorway surveying the slim girl before him, his expression as enigmatic as ever. His dark eyes beneath their heavy lids roamed slowly over the long blonde hair which rippled down the back of her thin, sleeveless pink silk blouse, tucked into a matching pair of slim trousers.

Sara coloured under his intense gaze and nervously twisted the new wedding ring on her finger.

'I'm sorry—I'm looking dreadful. I'm still not feeling very well, and . . .'

'I agree,' he interrupted dryly. As she hung her head in dejection, he added, 'I agree that you have not been well. However, you will feel much better in the fresh air. As to how you look . . .' he paused, and gave her a wry grin, 'there are many adjectives that I might use, but "dreadful" is not one of them.'

He moved over to take her hand firmly in his. 'Come along. Believe me, you will feel better soon.'

Glancing up through her eyelashes at the tall figure standing so close, Sara was again overcome by the extraordinary effect Jabir seemed to have on her. Her heart began to thud, and a return of the breathless nervousness she always felt when in close proximity to him made her feel weak and dizzy. Unresisting, she allowed herself to be led up into the fresh air.

Later, leaning on the ship's rail and looking at the view before her, she turned and smiled ruefully at Jabir.

'You were absolutely right, of course. I do feel much better. Marvellous, in fact.' She took great gulps of fresh air. 'This breeze is wonderful, and the island—it is an island, isn't it?—it looks lovely. But where exactly are we?'

Jabir joined her at the rail as she turned back to drink in the scene before her. She saw that the yacht was moored at the end of a long jetty which protruded out from one end of a curved and sandy beach. A tall ruined tower nestled in a grove of sweet-smelling pine trees, the scent of which filled the air.

'The captain tells me that this is one of the Iles d'Hyères, which lie off the coast of France between Nice and Marseilles,' Jabir smiled down at her. 'When you became so sick, I told the captain to make for the nearest land and instructed John to complete all the necessary arrangements.'

'It's lovely. Who owns the island?'

'Well,' he gave a dry cough, 'I do—now.'

'You don't mean—you can't have just bought an island because I was seasick?' Sara looked at him in utter bewilderment.

'Well, yes. It looks very charming, don't you think?'

'Yes, of course I do. But—but, Jabir, what about the people who own this place?' She gazed at him in distress.

'John informs me that the island is deserted, and that the owner, a Parisian banker, was delighted to sell. Apart from that,' Jabir said dismissively, 'I have no further information at the moment. I merely told John to arrange matters, and he has acted accordingly.'

'But you can't just . . .'

'Don't be foolish, Sara. Of course I can—and have. This whole business is totally unimportant, you know. There was a problem, and it has been solved. There is nothing more to say.'

He took hold of her elbow and led her towards some soft chairs set under gay beach umbrellas, by the swimming pool.

'Sit down and rest in the shade for a while, Sara. Later you might feel like a swim, yes?'

'Yes, that would be nice,' she said in a small voice, still feeling stunned by such a display of wealth and power.

A servant hurried up with a jug of cool lemonade, and after handing her a glass, Jabir sat back and contemplated the lovely girl as she quietly sipped her drink. Her long heavy blonde curtain of hair hid most of her face from his view, but he noticed the troubled glances she cast his way from time to time.

'You have no need to worry about being seasick again,' he said. 'I am proposing that we stay moored here for a few more days, sleeping on board. We can explore the island or swim and sunbathe—whatever you prefer. When we leave, John will take the yacht back to Cannes, it is only a few hours' sailing time away. He will leave the helicopter here, and I will fly us back to the yacht when it has docked. I would not bother to return to Cannes, but I have already arranged to hold a party for you to meet some of my friends.'

'Oh, Jabir, I've really ruined everything, haven't I?' Sara said in a whisper. 'Maybe I won't be sick again? We could try and see if . . .'

'Oh no,' he laughed, and raised a hand in mock horror. 'Allah forbid that you should have to go through that experience again—or myself, for that matter! Believe me, I will be pleased to sell the yacht. Maybe a house in Switzerland would suit you better? We shall see.'

He put down his glass and stood up. 'Alas, I must go and do some work. I suggest that you have a quiet lazy day, and we will meet again for a small meal this evening.'

Sara gazed at his retreating figure in horrified fascination. He had bought her family hotel, Sara herself and an island—solely on what appeared to be whims of the moment. Now, merely because she had been seasick, it seemed as if he was going to sell this huge yacht and buy a house in Switzerland instead! Just what sort of man had she married?

Sara sat at her dressing table on the yacht, now firmly moored back in Cannes, and watched as the expert hands of Monsieur André arranged her hair.

How typical of Jabir, she thought wryly, to have flown

the world-famous hair-stylist down from Paris to the
yacht, just to set her hair for the party tonight. The
trouble is, she thought gloomily, I could get used to it,
and become as autocratic and arrogant as Jabir himself.
She sighed heavily.

'You do not like ze 'air style, Princess?' Monsieur
André looked at her unhappy face in the mirror.

'Oh—oh yes. It's fine,' she smiled hurriedly back at
him. 'It looks lovely, *très . . .*' she hunted for a suitable
word, *'très chic.'*

'Ah, *bon*!' he murmured as he returned to his work.

I only wish my life was *bon*, Sara thought with a
lump of depression. Everything had seemed to be going
well, that first full day on the island. After a good
night's sleep she had felt much stronger, and had joined
Jabir to spend the morning wandering through the
pinewoods together.

He had seemed reluctant to discuss his family
background in Assir, so she had persuaded him to talk
about his schooldays in England instead. For the first
time in their relationship she had begun to relax and
enjoy his company, laughing at his tall stories about the
culture shock of an English boarding school on a small
boy from Arabia.

At lunch time a picnic hamper, surrounded by
comfortable cushions, had been waiting for them on the
grassy interior of the small ruined castle.

'Now it's your turn,' Jabir had said as they sat down
to eat their cold chicken and salad. 'Tell me all about
yourself, Sara.'

'What do you want to know?' She glanced through
her eyelashes at his broad-shouldered, lounging figure.
'I . . . I thought that clever Prince Jabir had a large file
on me already.' She hadn't been sure how he would
respond to her teasing words, and was relieved to see
him smile.

'Touché, Sara! But consider how woefully inadequate
it has proved to be. Nothing about what a bad sailor
you are, for instance!' He helped himself to more salad.

'What I had in mind, when I asked the question, was a wish to know more about your ... er ... your past life. Have you always lived in the hotel?'

'As long as I can remember,' she replied promptly. 'Dad's parents were killed by a bomb during the war, and he was brought up by his old grandmother. He'd always lived in the hotel, of course, and so when he married my mother they had their own small flat there. Granny Morrison was a fearsome old martinet who refused to let go the reins. Dad always said that she paid him a salary just to keep him out of her way!'

She smiled in recollection. 'Granny was awful—I was terrified of her. It's strange, really. I've far more memories of her than of my mother. She ran the hotel with a rod of iron until the day she died—about fifteen years ago. My mother was driving her out to the country to see some equally old great-aunt,' Sara added, 'and they were both killed when their car collided with a lorry.'

'Ah, Sara, I am sorry.' Jabir's voice was warmly sympathetic. 'You were very young to lose your mother, yes?'

'I was about five. Too young to realise what an upheaval the death of my mother and taking on the hotel meant for poor Dad.' Sara paused to nibble her chicken leg. 'What I really mind—and I'm not sure if you will understand—is that I find it becomes harder and harder to remember what my mother was really like. Just sometimes, when I smell a perfume like the one she used to wear, then I can dimly remember her . . .'

'All memories are clouded by time, Sara,' he said gently. 'It happens to all of us. Sometimes, indeed, we can have no memories. My mother, for instance, died when I was born, so you are maybe more fortunate than I.'

'Oh, Jabir, I didn't know . . .'

'Of course not—there is no reason why you should.' He waved his hand dismissively. 'So, your father was left to run the hotel on his own?'

'Yes. It must have been an awful shock for him, he'd never done a real day's work in his life. As you can imagine, when he found himself in charge, he hadn't a clue how to run the hotel efficiently and practically went to pieces.'

Jabir was surprisingly sympathetic. 'It was, perhaps, somewhat late in his life for him to take on such an enterprise?'

Sara sat thinking pensively for a moment. 'I ... er ... I imagine that you have a good idea of how matters, were, in the hotel?' He nodded silently. 'Well, in that case, there's little point in pretending that Dad was any good at managing the place,' she said resolutely. 'In fact, he was hopeless.'

'But you came to his rescue, did you not, Sara? It was ... er ... made quite clear to me—and I imagine the other guests—that if one wished for anything to be done, one must see Miss Morrison. Although nothing, it would seem, could cure the tepid bathwater!' he added with a wry laugh.

Sara's face flushed as she glanced up quickly to meet the lazy, amused gleam in his eyes. 'Well, yes,' she gave him a reluctant grin. 'We could never afford to do anything about replacing the antiquated boiler, you see.'

Jabir handed her a basket of strawberries and a jug of cream. 'I imagine the state of the bathwater was the least of your problems—yes?' he prompted dryly.

'Well, it was important ... but of course, you're quite right. It's your headache now, Jabir, but until you've tried to manage a hotel, you've no idea of the multitude of problems which can arise. It's like trying to run a country—in miniature, of course,' Sara mused, idly stirring a strawberry around her plate. 'I can't remember when I first started trying to help Dad. I went to a day school, and I used to come home to the hotel and help out with the accounts in the evening, take a turn on the reception desk—that sort of thing. I was always in trouble for not doing my school homework, but there never seemed to be enough time.' She shrugged. 'Anyway, things just snowballed, somehow. I took on more and more, and in the end was practically running the place . . . or trying to.'

'Poor Sara,' he murmured sympathetically. 'I don't suppose it left you much time for a personal life—boy-friends, for instance. You must have had lots, surely?'

'Yes, I did—have boy-friends, I mean. But not "lots", just a few.'

'Were you serious about any of them?' Jabir asked. She glanced quickly at him, but his voice and facial expression conveyed nothing other than mild interest.

'No, not really. Quite honestly,' she strove to explain, 'trying to run the hotel and achieve some sort of order and system—well, it really didn't leave me much time for any social life.'

'If matters had . . . er . . . had been arranged differently, I am sure you would have made the hotel a success. It is therefore a fruitless exercise to blame yourself for any failure on your part, Sara,' he said kindly but firmly.

'Yes, I know. Still, it was a good preparation for life, Jabir. Trying to placate an angry chef or arbitrating between the chief housekeeper and the linen department, for instance, took a fair amount of diplomacy, I can tell you! As for some of the guests . . . you've no idea of how rude some of them could be. I learnt very early on in life to keep a smile on my face, however hard it might be, and give them the soft answer that's supposed to turn away wrath. Not that it always worked!' she laughed.

'The customer is always right?' Jabir smiled.

'Absolutely! It's the first and last rule of the hotel business. Sometimes I thought I would scream with frustration. Every hour of the day there seemed to be a new crisis. After that apprenticeship I've always thought that I could cope with anything that life threw at me—even marriage to you, Jabir.'

Sara gasped as her unguarded, careless words hung in

the air between them. 'I'm so sorry, I . . . I shouldn't have said that. I . . .' she blushed a deep crimson, staring apprehensively down at her nervously twisting fingers.

Jabir gave a low laugh. 'Why not?' he answered blandly. 'I well realise that our . . . er . . . our marriage has been a considerable upheaval for you—a dramatic change in your life. It has also become quite clear to me,' his voice hardened, 'that you have been so busy trying to look after your father and the hotel that you have given precious little thought to what you personally want out of life.'

'I never said that. I . . .' she protested.

'No, you are much too loyal to your father. However, your clear astonishment yesterday, that I should have bought an island for your pleasure and comfort—a small matter in the context of the life I lead—was a clear indication of how little you have thought about your own needs and desires.'

Sara glanced up quickly, confused not only by his words, but by the gleam in his dark, hooded eyes.

'You are clearly very adaptable, but such adaptability is only gained at a considerable personal cost. You must learn to be more selfish, my Sara.'

The warm, caressing tone of his voice was disturbing. I'm never going to be able to 'adapt' enough to consider lovemaking 'a normal bodily function', she told herself miserably. Her cheeks, still pale from her sickness, flushed again as she realised that now she was better, Jabir would soon be demanding his marital rights. An apprehensive lump of despair settled like lead in her stomach.

Jabir rose, stretching his limbs and looked thoughtfully at the unhappy, hunched figure of his wife. He walked over, helping her to rise from her cushion. Firmly holding both her hands in his, he pulled her gently towards him, their bodies almost touching. He gazed down at Sara's upturned face, whose fluttering eyelashes, flushed cheeks and soft trembling lips betrayed extreme nervousness.

'My dear Sara,' he said softly, 'you have no need to fear me. We started our married life—our intimate married life—on the wrong foot. Yes?'

She nodded silently. The nearness of his tall figure in slim, hip-hugging jeans and a short-sleeved cotton shirt, open at the neck to display the strong column of his tanned throat, was causing her stomach to flutter in the most alarming manner.

'So, we will spend the next few days just getting to know each other. Learning to become friends. You understand what I am saying?'

'Yes, Jabir,' she whispered, relieved and grateful for his tolerance and understanding.

'Good,' he said briskly. 'Now, we will put the plates back in the hamper, and go for a walk down on the beach.'

They spent the rest of the day strolling along the sea-shore of the island. 'It's been a lovely day, it really has,' Sara turned impulsively to smile at Jabir, as they returned to the yacht in the late afternoon.

'Allah willing, there will be many such days ahead of us, Sara,' he said as they walked contentedly back along the jetty.

But it seemed that Allah wasn't willing, she thought unhappily. For those were the last kind words she had had from Jabir. No sooner had they gone on board the yacht than John Morgan had hurried forward with an anxious look on his face, and Jabir had disappeared into his office, leaving her to dine alone that night.

She hadn't seen him again until late the following morning, when he found her lying on a chaise-longue by the swimming pool.

She hadn't heard his approach and turned, startled at his voice, as he said, 'I thought I would leave my office for a while, and join you for coffee.'

She put down the book she had been reading. 'It's such a lovely day,' she smiled, 'maybe we could have another picnic?'

He ignored her words and sat down on a chair as

Hamid arrived with a tray. Jabir poured some coffee from a brass pot and placed a small handleless cup on the table beside her. Sara picked it up and looked doubtfully down at the greeny-brown liquid.

'Coffee drinking is an important part of our Bedouin tradition. What you have in your hand,' he said in a hard, impersonal voice, 'is a mixture of roasted coffee beans and cardamom seeds crushed together, and then infused with boiling water. It is our national drink—try it,' he added in a steely tone.

Sara hesitated, confused by the change in her husband, then raised the tiny cup to her lips. She took one sip and then another. The sharp, aromatic tang was not unpleasant, and she accepted a second cup.

A heavy silence stretched between them. Sara flushed as his hooded eyes roamed over her long legs topped by a brief pair of shorts, his expression grim and implacable.

Jabir stood up. 'You may spend the next few days as you wish,' he said coldly. 'You will be free to do what you like, except that you will have two hours' tuition every day from a member of my staff, in Arabic.'

'Arabic? You want me to learn Arabic?' She was confused. 'But I—I don't see . . .'

'What you see or do not see is unimportant,' he told her in a hard voice. 'All that is necessary for you to know is that I wish you to learn the language of my country. Do I make myself clear?'

'Yes, Jabir,' she whispered. The thick curtain of blonde hair falling from her bowed head hid her burning face from his view.

He sighed as he looked down at his new wife. Reluctantly, and in a softer tone, he said, 'I am not used to having my orders questioned. However, I have been in communication with my family. My father has . . . has expressed a desire to see you. We leave for Assir on our return to Cannes. It would, therefore, please me if you were able to greet him in Arabic.'

'Of course, I'll try.' Sara looked up, but he had gone as silently as he had arrived.

The next few days were lonely ones for Sara, as she sunbathed, walked in the pinewood, and struggled with her Arabic tuition. She saw very little of Jabir, except for the evening meal, where they were unable to talk freely because of the servants; and true to his word he never attempted to open the door which connected the bedrooms.

There was obviously something wrong with her husband. It might have been something she had inadvertently said, but she was sure, in fact, that it was to do with his family in Assir. It was after he had been in communication with them that he had become so distant and unfriendly. Whatever the cause, she felt incredibly lonely and homesick, and unable to enjoy what should have been the holiday of a lifetime.

She had bumped into John Morgan one afternoon by the sun deck, and swallowing her pride, had asked him outright what was wrong with Jabir.

He had looked extremely uncomfortable at her question. 'See here, Princess, it's not really my place to say anything—really it isn't.'

'Oh, John—please!' she begged.

'Well, for heaven's sake don't let the Prince know. 'It's . . .' he hesitated, '. . . it's the King.'

'The King? Jabir's father, you mean? What's happened? Is he all right?'

'Oh sure, he's fine. He's just hit the roof, that's all. Cables, telex—the lot. His language . . . wow! I tell you, the old boy's got a great command of the English language.'

'But why?' She suddenly felt cold. 'It's me, isn't it?' John's embarrassed silence confirmed her fears. 'It's because he's married me—that's why!'

'Now honey . . . er . . . Princess,' John sought to reassure her, 'believe me, it's not that simple. First off, it's nothing personal. It's just that the King had other plans for the Prince, that's all. He's a stubborn old guy by all accounts, and doesn't like to be thwarted.'

Sara stared at him in silence for a moment. Had Jabir married her because he wanted a good hostess and a mother for his children—or had he married her to forestall or block some plan of his father's? Either way, her position looked far worse than she could possibly have ever imagined.

'Why did he marry me? Why on earth did he do it?' she burst out in a sudden fury.

'Look, the Prince is just as tough and stubborn as his old dad. No one, but no one, tells him what to do, and that includes his father. He wanted to marry you, so he did. Don't go looking for problems where there are none.'

'What plans did his father have for Jabir?' she asked anxiously.

'Oh no! There's no way I'm going into that! It's all bound up with internal family politics in Assir, and that's a very complicated kettle of fish, well outside my brief. I never go to Assir. I'm only concerned with the Prince's business in the West.'

And try as she might, Sara had been unable to get John to say any more on the subject.

The journey by helicopter, back to the yacht in Cannes that morning, had been conducted virtually in silence. Jabir had been taciturn, and she was feeling far too upset and nervous to say anything.

As she sat watching Monsieur André place the last curl in position, Sara was in a considerable state of mental exhaustion. So much so that later in the evening, while their guests were arriving, she was still standing ready dressed in her room when Jabir arrived, looking angry.

'Why aren't you in the salon ready to receive our guests? Some of them have come aboard already.'

Sara, staring out of the window at the lights of Cannes, spun around as he spoke, and raised her blue eyes, wide with fright, to his face.

'Oh, Jabir! I think I've—I've got stage fright, or something . . .'

'Don't be so foolish, Sara. It's really no different from a reception in your hotel.'

'I know—I know! Don't you think I've been telling myself that for the past hour? It's all right for you, you'll know everyone there. They're all your friends. But me . . .? Even you don't want to talk to me. These last few days have been absolute hell! I . . . I've never been so lonely and miserable in all my life,' she wailed. 'It's no good, Jabir, I just can't go in there . . . I can't!'

Jabir looked at his wife. Her golden hair was swept up, and formed a plaited coronet on the top of her head. Her bare shoulders, gleaming in the lamplight, rose from a deep frill of white silk chiffon, edged with lace. A wide blue band emphasised her slender waist, from which the fully gathered white chiffon skirt broke in soft folds to just below her knees. She wore no jewellery, except for his diamond necklace, and would have looked spectacularly beautiful, if she hadn't looked so terrified.

Groaning with impatience, Jabir strode over to stand in front of her. 'My virgin bride! We can't have people meeting you in this state,' he said decisively, and before she realised his intention he grasped her tightly in his arms. His firm lips descended on hers, and instinctively she tried to push him away. Ignoring her desperate fluttering hands, his mouth began to invade hers, with an exploring kiss, the like of which she had never known.

Sara's senses began to swim, she felt she was falling into a deep abyss as the burning pressure of his mouth ignited a stirring flame within her. Slowly, and involuntarily, totally unaware of what she was doing, she arched her body closer to his. Her arms encircled his neck, and she moaned softly as his hand firmly possessed the warm curve of her breast.

Her entire being seemed to be dissolving in a molten heap of desire, when Jabir abruptly released her from

his embrace. Sara would have fallen without the
support of his arm around her waist. He looked down
at her swollen lips, her eyes still glowing with
languorous desire, and gave a short, dry laugh.

'You may be late in receiving our guests tonight,
Sara. But no one present will have any doubts as to
exactly what has delayed you!'

Her legs felt as if they were made of cotton wool,
as Jabir led her unresisting along the corridor to the
salon, already filling up with a bright, chattering
throng. As they moved through the room, greeting his
friends, they presented a charming picture of married
bliss.

The party was a great success, and Jabir's stratagem
had obviously worked—if the envious glances cast her
way by some of the beautiful women present were any
guide.

The evening drew to a close, and Jabir came back
into the salon from bidding farewell to the last of his
guests. Sara was standing with her back to him as he
approached, staring blindly at one of the oil paintings
on the wall.

'Sara,' he said quietly, 'I'm sorry. I had to do
something—for your own sake.'

Sara's tortured nerves snapped, and she turned on
him bitterly. 'Oh no! Not for my sake—for *yours*! You
couldn't let it be known that your wife was anything
but blissfully happy, could you? People simply don't
matter to you, it's just a matter of cheques and
balances. Is this good value? Will I get a better return
for that? You bought me—I hope you think it's worth
it!'

Jabir stood looking silently at the unhappy girl, his
face a blank mask.

'You must have had a good laugh,' Sara continued,
torturing herself. 'You wound me up, just like a
clockwork doll, to exactly the right pitch, didn't you?
God knows why you married me, Jabir—I certainly
don't. It's just your bad luck that I'm flesh and blood,

and not . . . not a calculating machine like yourself!' She
burst into a flood of tears.

'You are merely tired and overwrought, Sara,' Jabir
replied in a firm, hard voice, taking a large
handkerchief from his pocket and handing it to her.
'Come, dry your tears. Upon reflection you will come
to see that I have merely wounded your pride—and for
that I apologise.'

'I don't want or need your damned apology,' Sara
cried angrily, sniffing and blowing her nose. He hadn't
apologised for . . . for kissing her the way he had, she
noticed, glancing at the tall, stiff figure of her husband.
Oh God, just what sort of marriage have I got myself
into? she groaned inwardly, for the hundredth time.

With an effort she pulled herself together. 'However,
you're quite right, Jabir. I am tired. I'm so tired that I
. . . I just don't care any more—about anything. Just . . .
just leave me alone in future, that's all I ask.' She
turned her face away from the hard, searching look in
his hooded dark eyes. 'Please . . . just leave me alone!'

'Sara! I . . .' his voice grated harshly in the large,
empty room.

'I . . . I don't want to discuss the matter any more!'
she cried, running swiftly from the room.

CHAPTER FOUR

'Jabir! Oh, Jabir! You've come in time for my wedding—I knew you would!' A small, dark, petite figure threw herself into Jabir's arms as he stepped out of the black Cadillac, which had come to a halt in the courtyard of the Palace complex.

He laughed and kissed the young girl, before turning to help Sara, who was struggling to follow him. Her progress was hampered by the cloudy weight of the thin black veiling she had been asked to wear for the drive from the airport.

The girl put her arms around Sara and gave her a hug. 'Welcome! Welcome to Assir. Let me take that horrid old *aba* off—you don't need it here.' Sara was grateful to be relieved of the veil, and stood blinking in the strong sunlight, smiling at the girl in front of her.

'Sara, this is my thoroughly disreputable young sister, Hassa. How she ever managed to find a husband ...' Jabir shook his head in mock horror.

'Oh, poof!' Hassa took Sara's hand and started chattering as she led her towards a large building of honey-coloured stone, covered in trailing vines. 'Ever since we heard about Jabir's marriage, I've been longing to see you. You're so *beautiful*, Nurra will be terribly jealous! Did you have a good flight? My mother is terribly excited and curious ...'

'Enough! Enough, Hassa!' Jabir laughed as he accompanied them up the marble steps of the building. 'We've only just got off the plane, give us time to catch our breath!'

The large, cool hall was refreshing after the searing heat outside, and Sara looked around her with interest. It was very formal, with the minimum of furniture, its lofty ceiling painted in delicate tones of the softest pink and grey, matching a large and sumptuous Persian carpet, lying like a velvet pool on the marble floor.

At their entry, an enormous crowd of servants erupted into the hall and began to sway and eddy about them, the air filled with high-pitched joyful voices saluting their master's return. Men in white robes with red and white cloths secured by black ropes on their heads fought to catch and kiss Jabir's hands. Sara, who had been battling with her Arabic lessons for the past few days, knew, with total conviction, that she would never be able to understand, let alone speak, such an incomprehensible language. She shivered involuntarily, struck by a sudden chill of loneliness, as she stood an alien Western figure amidst such an Eastern environment.

The noise and bustle mounted to a crescendo, which was brought to an abrupt and sudden halt by a clap of Jabir's hands.

There was an instant silence as most of the servants melted away about their business, as swiftly and quickly as they had arrived.

'Shall I take Sara to her suite? She'll want to freshen up after the journey,' said Hassa, as she directed the remaining servants to take Jabir and Sara's cases upstairs.

'Yes, of course.' Jabir removed his headcovering as he turned to have a word with Hamid, then started to mount the wide staircase. 'I'll be in the schoolroom with the children, so don't be too long.'

'Oh, how lovely!' was Sara's involuntary cry, as she stood in the doorway, surveying her new bedroom, decorated in white and pale lemon, the same shades as the sitting room through which they had just passed, the gauze curtains billowing in the breeze from the open windows.

'I'm so glad you like it. I had a word with Ahmad, Jabir's major-domo, before you arrived. He apparently had a terrific job to get everything ready in time. He wasn't told why he had to complete your suite in three weeks, and as you know decorators seem to spend for ever . . .'

'Three weeks?' Sara looked at the girl in surprise.

'Yes—not long, was it?' Hassa continued to chatter as Sara was struck by the chilling realisation of just how certain of her agreement to their marriage Jabir had been.

'Here's your bathroom, and this door leads to Jabir's suite . . .' Hassa darted around, opening doors, as Sara's head began to ache. It had been a long flight from Cannes, and she looked at the bed with longing. However, she had to meet her new stepchildren first, but not hot and sticky like this.

'Is there time for me to have a quick shower, Hassa?' she asked.

'Yes, of course. I see the servants have brought up your luggage. I'll be in your sitting room when you're ready.'

Standing under the refreshing spray of the water, Sara recalled their arrival at Assir's airport. She had been told to remain in the plane while Jabir had donned a white headcloth—a *kaffiyeh*—secured by two bands of gold rope. His headdress should have looked incongruous with his dark linen suit, but Sara thought he looked extremely handsome, as she saw him run down the steps from the aircraft.

Watching from inside the jet, she noticed that various men came up to greet him, and was startled to see them bow and kiss his hand. A brass band began to play as he inspected a small guard of honour. Sara knew that she had married into an Arabian royal family, but she hadn't realised that there would be this kind of pomp and circumstance. Oh well, 'When in Rome . . .' she thought, and stood patiently as the stewardess helped to cover her with a voluminous black veil which reached down to her ankles.

Following that terrible row after the party on the yacht, she and Jabir had hardly exchanged more than brief polite words with each other. He had issued the necessary instructions for their journey in a bland, impersonal voice, and she had acquiesced silently to his commands. On the flight to Assir, she had sat miserably huddled in her large chair, dozing and studiously ignoring her husband.

However, as, unaccustomed to the veil's usage, she had stumbled down the aircraft steps, she noticed that Jabir had been unable to repress a faint grin at her clumsiness.

'It's all right for you!' she muttered angrily, as she endeavoured to follow him into the waiting limousine. Unfortunately, at that moment her foot caught on the veiling and she found herself catapulted forward into Jabir's arms.

'It's very nice for me,' he said in an amused voice, as he embraced the slim shrouded figure of his wife.

'Oh, Jabir, it's not funny. Please help me, I can't cope with this . . .' Sara pleaded, abandoning any attempt to maintain her dignity as she struggled with the enveloping black material.

'Come, just sit still, and I will sort this out,' he said, helping her to sit back comfortably against the seat.

'I feel like a huge black widow spider,' she moaned, as Jabir bent down to retrieve her handbag from the floor where she had dropped it.

'On the contrary, I find it very alluring to see you dressed so. It is only the first time you have worn the veil—it will become easier in future,' he assured her.

As they left the airport and drove through the suburbs of Assir's capital city Jabir, clearly disposed to be friendly, pointed out places of interest. Architecturally modern buildings of all shapes and sizes flashed by as they drove down a wide highway beside the sea, the small flag on the front of the car fluttering in the breeze. They passed through an archway with sentries on either side, and down an avenue of what Jabir said were tamarisk trees, before reaching another gateway with castellated walls either side, and more sentries, who jerked to attention as they passed.

Once inside the walls of the Palace grounds, she was struck by the greenness of it all. Lawns, large flowering shrubs and tall trees—it seemed like an oasis from the dusty road along which they had travelled.

She had felt a lump of nervous anticipation at the unknown life ahead of her, and was therefore relieved to find Jabir's sister so unexpectedly helpful and friendly.

Ten minutes later, showered and changed into a simple cotton dress, Sara felt better. She was sitting at her dressing table, brushing her long hair, when Hassa returned.

'Oh, Sara, you're so lucky to be so beautiful—no wonder Jabir fell madly in love with you! I'd give anything to have your lovely hair.'

'Well, I think I look very ordinary,' she said, sighing inwardly at Hassa's romantic illusions. 'In fact, I'd much prefer to have hair like yours.' She smiled at the young girl's dusky curls.

Hassa laughed and sat down on a chair. 'No one's ever satisfied with themselves, are they?' She paused. 'By the way, Sara, please don't take any notice of me. I'm always talking nineteen to the dozen, but I do hope we will be friends. It's going to be such fun having you here.'

'I'm sure we'll be great friends,' Sara replied. 'As you can imagine, it all seems very strange, and I'll be very glad of any help you can give me.

'We've only got a few minutes now, but maybe we can get together later, and have a really good gossip.' Hassa got up excitedly and went over to perch on the windowsill. 'I'm dying to show you my wedding dress! It's only two weeks to the wedding, and you must give me lots of hints on how to be a good wife—there's so much about married life that I don't know.'

You're not the only one, thought Sara gloomily, and made a determined effort to change the subject. 'Do you live here in this palace, Hassa?'

'This isn't really the Palace, it's Jabir's house. There

are many houses like this in the Palace complex,
although they're not all as large as this one, of
course. We also have a small school for all the
children, and a private mosque. We're a very large
family, you know. I think it came to about five
hundred at the last count.' Hassa giggled at Sara's
amazed expression. 'It's all right, they don't all live
here—just the immediate family. For instance, the
house over there,' Hassa pointed behind her, out of
the window. 'That belongs to the widow of my
brother Muhammed. He was two years older than
Jabir, but he was very wild and absolutely mad on
aeroplanes. He crashed his plane into a mountain a
year ago,' she explained sadly.

'I'm so sorry . . .' Sara murmured.

'Anyway,' Hassa gave herself a shake, 'my father's
house, the only building referred to as a palace, is set
back across the big lawn, overlooking the sea. It's the
oldest part of this set of buildings and consists mainly
of a large square block containing the formal reception
rooms, and separate private family wings. I live there
with my mother, the Queen, and brother Fahad, who is
eighteen. My other brothers and sisters are away
abroad at school at the moment.'

She rose. 'I'd better stop chatting and take you along
to the schoolroom now, if you're ready.'

With a swift, reassuring glance in her mirror, Sara
got up to follow the girl. I do hope Jabir's little girls like
me, she prayed silently, as they walked along the wide
corridor. Hassa, an ever-ready mine of information,
told Sara how much the children missed their father
during his long absences abroad.

'The children must miss their mother too,' said Sara
sympathetically.

Hassa didn't answer, as she opened the door of the
schoolroom for Sara, and then left to run down the
stairs, calling over her shoulder, 'See you for lunch!'

Jabir was sitting on a sofa with a little girl perched on
his knees, either side of him. He looked up as Sara

entered the room, and gently detached the children's arms from around his neck.

'Come and meet your new mother,' he said, leading the children forward.

'How do you do, stepmother,' said the elder of the two girls, as she shook Sara's hand and curtsied. Her smaller sister did the same, stumbling over the words, as they looked solemnly at their father's new wife.

Sara could not contain her warm-hearted sympathy for the two little motherless children, and she dropped on to one knee and took their hands in hers.

'Please ... please call me Sara, won't you? "Stepmother" sounds awful, and I really don't feel quite that old yet!' Her gentle laugh sparked a timorous answering smile from the elder girl, Nadia, but the younger child turned to look up at Jabir with anxious eyes.

'Will you show me around the house tomorrow?' Sara asked Nadia. 'It's all so new to me, and without your help I won't know where to go.'

Nadia nodded, and smiled.

'Good—I'll look forward to that,' said Sara, rising from the floor as Jabir said, '. . . And this is Miss Scott, who brought us all up, and now looks after the girls. We led you a hell of a life, didn't we, Scotty?'

'That's quite enough of your cheek, Master Jabir! Using words like that—whatever next?'

Sara turned smiling to greet Miss Scott, and was shaken to find the old nanny staring at her dumbfounded, as if she'd seen a ghost.

'Are you all right, Scotty?' asked Jabir, instantly concerned.

'Och, I'm fine dear, just fine. Just a wee turn. I expect it's the heat.'

Miss Scott, who was well named—her homeland was obvious from her Scottish burr—walked forward, smiling warmly at Sara with approval.

'Well, I'm glad to see he's had the sense to find himself a bonny lass at last,' she said, taking Sara's hands, and giving her a kiss. 'I hope you'll both be very happy. Just you make sure, dearie, that you keep him in order. He can be a very naughty boy—far too fond of getting his own way.'

Sara managed to keep a straight face until they left the room. Then she started to laugh weakly as she accompanied Jabir down the marble staircase. 'Me, keep you in order? That'll be the day!'

'Oh, I don't know . . .' Jabir, completely unabashed, looked up smiling from the step below her, as he turned and took her hand, raising it to his lips. The touch of his warm mouth on the palm of her hand sent nervous tremors coursing through her veins, and the unmistakable gleam in his hooded eyes made her heart beat furiously.

He dropped her hand abruptly, and turning, ran down the marble steps. 'Come on, it's time for lunch. Hassa is joining us.'

Too tired and nervous to do anything but pick at her food, Sara sat back and watched as Jabir and Hassa laughed and talked together. She despaired of ever being able to understand her husband. He seemed to be a totally different person here, in his own country, from the austere ruthless businessmen she had married. He obviously adored his children and had a friendly and warm relationship with Hassa.

As brother and sister traded laughing insults across the table, Sara sighed inwardly. As far as she could see, apart from that happy day on the island, she had had little but indifference and rejection from Jabir. He just picked her up and used her, as he had the night of the party in Cannes, and then promptly dropped her again. Weary and depressed, she wished he would be half as kind and pleasant to her as he was to Hassa.

Sara had been so immersed in her miserable thoughts that it wasn't until she heard her own name mentioned that she paid any attention to the conversation between Hassa and Jabir.

' . . . you and Sara. However, my dear brother,'

Hassa laughed, 'you are definitely *persona non grata* until tomorrow. Father is going off hunting in the desert tomorrow evening, and so he has relented sufficiently to announce that he will receive you both in audience, to be followed by a lunch for the family. He's calmed down a lot really—considering the circumstances.'

What circumstances? thought Sara. It's all so confusing, I wish I knew what was going on.

'However,' Hassa added in a warning tone, 'as you can imagine, there is *one* member of the family who is . . . er . . . not at all happy.'

Jabir looked searchingly at his sister for a moment, his face a blank mask. 'Ah—yes,' he said slowly, putting down his napkin and rising from the table. 'You must excuse us, Hassa. Sara looks tired and should rest.'

'Of course,' said his sister. 'I'll call and see you later some time, Sara.'

'You look exhausted,' Jabir said roughly, escorting her firmly upstairs to her bedroom. 'I want you to rest for the remainder of the day. If you need anything just ring for your maid. I am giving orders that you are not to be disturbed.'

He hesitated, as she stood beside him, swaying with fatigue. Very slowly, he placed an arm around her shoulders and pulled her gently so as to lean against his tall figure.

'My poor Sara! It has been a terrible week for you, hasn't it? When you are feeling less tired, we will talk. We will talk calmly, yes?'

She nodded wearily, her face buried against his shoulder.

'Good. Now,' he said releasing her, 'I must leave you. Rest well, you will feel better soon.'

He's a complete enigma, she thought as she lay dozing on her bed. Most of the time he's hard, tough and ruthless, and then suddenly he's kind and considerate. I wish—I wish I could understand him better . . .

She slept like a log for some hours and awoke to find the late afternoon sun stealing in through the gauze curtains. Slipping out of bed, she went to the window. The day was cooler now, servants were watering the trees and shrubs in the Palace gardens, and a sweet-scented perfume arose from the flowers on the climbing plant which covered the large house.

Suddenly feeling thirsty, she rang the bell for Yashi, her new maid, who soon returned with a jug of cold lemonade, before helping Sara to unpack and put away her clothes in the large wardrobes.

Later, sitting in a comfortable chair by the open window, Sara slowly sipped her drink and tried to think positively about her new life. It wasn't easy.

In the midst of her depressing thoughts, there was a knock, and Hassa put her head around the door.

'Yashi said you were awake . . .?'

'Yes, do come in,' called Sara, relieved to see her cheerful face. Hassa's bubbling personality was sure to help her forget, even if only momentarily, the unhappy doubts and fears about her marriage.

'I suddenly thought that you might be wondering about what to wear while you're here in Assir. Is there any advice I can give you?'

'Oh, Hassa, that's really kind of you. I wasn't at all sure. Yashi's hung my things in the wardrobes, have a look and tell me what you think.'

'Gosh! You've got some super dresses—and all those shoes dyed to match!' Hassa sighed enviously.

'But are they suitable for Assir?' Sara asked anxiously. 'I thought they were all too "grand" in London, but Jabir insisted . . .'

'Oh, you know us Arabs,' Hassa laughed in self-mockery. 'We can't have too much of a good thing. This dress, for instance, will be perfect for any evening party. Very bridal!'

She held up the heavy cream satin dress against herself, swaying in front of the mirror, as its silver bead and pearl embroidery caught the light. 'What a pity you're so much taller—and slimmer—than I am, otherwise I'd pinch the lot.' She put the dress away reluctantly, and came over to sit beside Sara.

'Clotheswise, anything goes here in the Palace grounds, although swimsuits and bikinis are only permitted in the private swimming pools of the houses.'

'What about having to wear a veil?' asked Sara.

'My father is fairly old-fashioned, and he likes the women of the family to wear a veil—an *aba*—when we go out in the streets, either in a car or on foot. You won't be compelled to wear a veil in the streets if you don't want to, but it would be sensible to wear a dress with long sleeves. Visiting Bedouin from the desert would be terribly shocked if you didn't. You see, there's still a big divide between the townsfolk and the desert tribes, and there's little point in upsetting people, is there?'

Yashi entered with a fresh jug of lemonade as Hassa added, 'You won't find it too difficult—really. The old harem idea has died out, and women are free to come and go as they please.'

'You've been a great help, Hassa,' said Sara. 'I must admit I was worried about exactly what to wear here. I mean, all those stories about women shut away in harems, never allowed to meet men . . .'

Hassa gave a peal of laughter, and Sara grinned at the girl. 'It's all very well laughing, but it's obviously quite a different life here from the one I led in London. Jabir is no use at all. He just shrugs his shoulders and says, "All will become clear" . . .'

A note of bitterness in her voice caused Hassa to frown with concern. 'You are happy with Jabir, aren't you? I mean, you do love each other, truly?'

Inwardly cursing herself for having nearly let slip the truth about her marriage, Sara hastened to reassure the girl.

'Of course we're happy . . . very happy indeed. It's just that . . . that we've only been married a week, and there's so much I don't know about your family, and Arabian customs.'

'I'm so glad,' said Hassa. 'Jabir is absolutely my favourite brother. He's had a lot of unhappiness in his life, and I'm so glad that he now has you to love him and make him happy.'

'He must have been shattered when his wife died,' Sara said slowly. 'Jabir's never said anything. How did it happen? I don't mean to pry, but I don't want to upset him by asking.'

Hassa looked embarrassed. 'I'm sorry, Sara. I would help you if I could—I really would. But Jabir never talks about it, and he has forbidden any mention of the subject in the family.' She looked miserably at Sara. 'I'm really sorry. You'll have to ask him all about it yourself.'

Sara was puzzled, but she hastened to reassure Hassa. 'Of course I will. I shouldn't have asked you. I'm sorry.' She paused, then took the plunge.

'Jabir's father is apparently very upset at our marriage. Is that also a forbidden subject?'

'Not as far as I know,' answered Hassa with a grin. 'The family has talked about nothing else since we received a cable to say he was married.'

'Didn't he tell anyone beforehand?'

'No—not a dicky-bird, as Scotty would say! And that's what has really upset my father. He and Jabir are very alike, you know, tough on the top but really very mushy underneath.'

Sara blinked at a description of her husband that she found hard to believe.

'You've absolutely no need to worry,' Hassa continued at full spate. 'Father's going to love you— you're so beautiful.'

'I believe he had . . . er . . . other plans,' said Sara as carelessly as she could, pouring them both a drink.

'Yes, and aren't we all relieved about that! The thought of Nurra and Jabir was really more than I could stomach. My mother has been very discreet about the whole thing, but I know she's pleased too. Nurra's as mad as fire, and when she sees you, she'll be green

with envy.' Hassa gave a wide grin. 'Honestly—I can't
wait until tomorrow. I really can't!'

'You mean . . .? You mean your father is angry
because he wanted Jabir to marry someone called
Nurra?' Sara said slowly.

'Yes, of course, but there's no need to worry, I . . .'
Hassa looked at Sara with dawning horror.

'*Wallahi*,' she groaned, 'my big mouth! You didn't
know, did you?'

'No, I didn't, but it's about time someone told me
what's going on,' Sara said grimly. 'Now, Hassa, just
who is Nurra?'

'She's the widow of Muhammed, Jabir's older
brother. I told you about him this morning, if you
remember. He died last year in a plane crash.' She
gestured to the window. 'Nurra lives in the house over
there.'

'Why would your father want Jabir to marry his
brother's widow?'

'Frankly, Sara, for political reasons, mainly. Her father
is a Sultan in the north of the country and wields a lot of
power. Besides which, he is also bad-tempered and
difficult. Jabir's marriage to Nurra would have solved a
lot of problems for my father, no doubt about that.'

'You said Nurra was angry?' Sara took a deep
breath. 'Do I take it that Jabir has been . . . er . . .
consoling her in her widowhood?'

Hassa blushed. 'Sara, in all honesty, I don't know.
To be fair, I don't like Nurra, so I've been quite
prepared to think the worst,' she admitted. Their
conversation was interrupted by a squeal of brakes in
the drive outside. Hassa got up and went to lean out of
the window.

'Jabir's back,' she said, 'and it's time I went home
anyway.' She looked doubtfully at Sara. 'I hope I
haven't said anything to upset you?'

'Certainly not,' Sara said firmly. 'Thanks to you, I do
at least have some idea of what's going on. I'm grateful,
believe me.'

She sat quietly looking out of the window after Hassa had gone. Her new sister-in-law had given her quite a lot to think about, none of it particularly comforting.

Her thoughts were interrupted by the entrance of Jabir, dressed casually in riding breeches and shiny black long leather boots, his open-necked white shirt seeming to fit his wide shoulders like a glove, while the rolled-up sleeves displayed his muscular arms.

She flushed and caught her breath as his tall figure lounged against the open door, radiating a powerful aura of strong and virile masculinity.

'I've just been visiting my stud farm and I feel like cooling off with a swim. I was wondering whether you would care to join me.'

'Yes ... er ...' Sara tried to pull her errant thoughts together, under the lazy amused gaze of her husband. 'Yes, I'd love to. Does—does it matter what I wear?' she added, thinking about the advice given to her by Hassa.

'As little as possible, of course,' he replied in a bland voice, and continued in the same tone, 'I have a few telephone calls to make first, so ask your maid to direct you to the pool. I will join you there as soon as I can.' He turned to leave, before being struck by a sudden thought. 'I am assuming that you can swim, Sara?'

'Oh yes,' she said, nettled by his impersonal attitude. 'Just because I was sick on that ocean-going liner of yours, it doesn't mean I can't swim.'

'Good,' he grinned. 'I'll see you later, then.'

I know I've got a one-piece bathing suit here somewhere, Sara thought nervously, as she hunted through her chest of drawers. 'As little as possible' indeed! There was no way she was going into that pool in a skimpy bikini—not with Jabir there. The thought of his heavy-lidded glance, and the way his eyes always raked over her figure, made her feel quite sick with apprehension. However, as she surveyed herself in the mirror a few minutes later, she felt much calmer.

Admittedly, she thought as she tried to hitch it up,

the square front of her black swimsuit was cut rather low. Very low, in fact, she realised with dismay as she regarded the plainly visible swell of her full breasts. Nevertheless, it was certainly far more decent than anything else she possessed. Or was it? She stood hesitating for a moment, then shrugged helplessly. It would have to do.

Later, as she floated gently in the pool, Sara felt more relaxed than she had for some days. Vines and climbing shrubs, with bright red and lilac flowers, covered the walls of the swimming pool enclosure, and she felt cool and refreshed as she slowly absorbed the atmosphere of peace and quiet. She smiled as she remembered Hassa's words, about Arabs not being able to have too much of a good thing. The pool itself was enormous and the diving platforms were, in her experience, well up to competition standard.

Hearing a noise, she flipped over to see Jabir standing by the wide steps which led into the water at the shallow end of the pool. She began to swim lazily towards him, her hair tied in a ponytail floating behind her.

He undid his towelling wrap and threw it on to an adjacent chair, before walking slowly down the steps. Sara paused to tread water as she looked at the lean hard body advancing towards her. His tanned skin rippled over the powerful muscles of his torso, and his dark swimming trunks were brief enough to display a hard flat stomach over strong hard thighs.

Her body and face suddenly felt unaccountably hot, and she somersaulted in the water before swimming away to the deep end of the pool. A few moments later he surfaced beside her, as she clung to the rail, striving to regain her composure.

'Are you enjoying yourself?' he asked, shaking the water from his head.

'It's lovely—but what a huge pool,' she said breathlessly.

'I like to swim to keep fit, but I find it very boring to

have to keep turning around at each end. I therefore told the architect to build me as long a pool as possible.'

'And the diving structure . . .?'

'Ah!' he grinned sheepishly. 'I was abroad at the time, and I'm afraid the architect got rather carried away!'

They both smiled at each other, and Sara was suddenly very conscious of the nearness of his body, the heavy gold chain with a gold medallion lying amidst the black curly hairs on his chest, and of the glint in his dark eyes as they rested on the swell of her breasts clearly displayed by the low cut front of her swimsuit.

As if sensing her nervousness, he said, 'Come, I will race you to the other end and back.'

'Don't I get a head start?' she asked demurely, smiling at him from beneath lowered lashes. 'It doesn't seem very fair.'

Jabir put his head on one side, as he noticed her soft lips curved into a small, secret smile. 'Now, Sara, it is not like you to be coy . . .' He let go of the rail to put an arm about her slim waist, pressing her to him, and looking down into her face. 'What are you up to, I wonder?'

'Up to?' she queried breathlessly, as they floated in the water together, his face only inches from her own.

'My instincts about you are very seldom wrong,' he said slowly, his arm tightening about her waist for a moment, before he let her go. 'However, we will see. Now, let's have a race—the exercise will do you good.'

'If you tell me once more that something "will do me good" I'll . . . I'll . . .!' she snapped at him, disturbed and upset by their close encounter.

'What will you do, my Sara?' he laughed.

'I'll win this race for a start!' she yelled as she catapulted herself forward through the water in a lithe fast crawl. The suppressed anger and frustration she had been feeling since Jabir had decided to marry her lent her body wings, as she flew through the water. She could feel him closing up fast behind, and swung into a racing turn before ploughing her way back down the pool again.

Touching the end first, she turned to see Jabir only three yards away, and a moment later he was beside her. They both held to the rail panting and trying to catch their breath.

'I knew you were up to something! And yes, I see you can swim, very well indeed!' he said with a grin, climbing up on to the side, before leaning down and helping Sara out of the pool. 'Where did you learn to swim like that?'

He's a good loser, she thought in pleased surprise as she went over to pick up her towel. 'Well,' she said, drying her face, 'I liked swimming and joined a club in London when I was small. I used to swim in inter-club competitions until I got too old.'

'Too old? At twenty years of age you are too old?' he laughed.

'At twenty, you're positively ancient nowadays! No, at about fourteen my body started to develop and . . .' she blushed and hurriedly continued, ' . . . I found I was being beaten by twelve-year-olds. So I took up diving instead.'

'You can dive—on such as this?' Jabir indicated the structure behind him.

'Is it so surprising?' she replied, turning around to look for her wrap. His eyes had begun to gleam again at the sight of her slim figure in the wet, tight-fitting swimsuit, and she felt a return of the nervous tension he seemed to evoke so easily in her.

'From the top board? It is not possible,' he said dismissively.

'Oh, really?' Sara turned to look at her husband. 'Can it be that your precious dossier on me has let you down—again?' she asked, her voice dripping with sarcasm. 'Oh dear, dear me—poor Jabir, what a shame!' With a spurt of anger she threw her towel at him and ran swiftly along the side of the pool.

After a moment's surprise, he laughed and began to

run after her, stopping at the base of the diving tower, as she ran lightly up the ladder.

'Sara, come down at once! It is much too dangerous,' he called, the smile leaving his face as she climbed higher and higher.

'No,' she called back. 'You and your damn dossier . . . I'll show you!'

Standing on the top board, she felt a moment's apprehension. She was out of practice, and to dive from this height she really should have had some lower dives first. Well, she'd just have to concentrate—and get it right!

Jabir stepped back to watch her slim figure as she walked along the board. He opened his mouth to call to her to stop, then realised the danger in distracting her attention. He tensed as Sara stood balancing herself, flinching as he watched her launch herself up and forward with infinite grace. Falling downward, she twisted twice in the air before straightening out to cleave through the water, hardly making a ripple on the surface.

She surfaced and swam slowly towards the side of the pool, astounded to see from Jabir's white face and blazing eyes that he was very angry indeed. He pulled her roughly out and seizing her shoulders, shook her in a fury.

'Never, never do such a thing again!' he shouted at the dazed girl. 'You might have killed yourself! Promise me? Never again?'

'Yes . . . yes, all right, I promise. I . . . I'm sorry, Jabir.' Sara looked anxiously at him. 'I was quite safe, truly I was. It's a very simple dive, really it is. It only seems difficult.'

Jabir looked at her blankly for a moment, before letting her go. 'You . . . er . . . you frightened me,' he said, turning to hand her her wrap before picking up his towelling robe.

'I think we both need a drink,' he said blandly, leading the way to a small summer house set in the surrounding wall. Opening the doors, he went inside and walked over to a bar in the corner. 'May Allah forgive me, but I need this,' he said, pouring a large measure of brandy, and drinking it down in one gulp.

'Jabir, I'm sorry,' Sara said in a small voice. 'I think . . . I think I was showing off. It was very silly and stupid of me.' She shrugged in embarrassment and bit her lip. 'It's just . . . it's just that I always get so cross when I think of that dossier you had done on me. Can I . . . er . . . can I have a drink too?'

'Hubris,' said Jabir.

Sara looked uncomprehendingly at him.

'Hubris,' he repeated. 'The sin of pride. An old classics master at my school used to talk about it—with particular reference to myself, I'm sorry to say. You are a proud woman, Sara, and you resent the fact that I should have had a dossier compiled about you—a very bad one, as it turns out! It has hurt your pride. Yes?'

Looking down as she fiddled with her wedding ring, Sara nodded silently.

'I understand how you feel.' Jabir leaned over the bar and placed a hand gently under her chin, raising her face to meet his steady gaze. 'We will not refer to that document ever again—and you will also never again dive from the top board—promise me?'

'Never again,' she promised.

'In that case,' he said with a broad smile, 'we will celebrate with some champagne. Pull up a stool, Sara, while I play the part of barman.'

Sipping her drink, Sara suddenly realised that for the first time in their tortuous relationship she didn't feel as nervous and awkward with her husband as usual. Well, not quite as much, she amended quickly, as she felt his eyes regarding her steadily over his glass.

'Jabir,' she said quietly, 'you should have told me that your father is upset that you married me.'

There was a long silence before he spoke. 'I won't ask where you heard about it—Hassa, I suppose.' He sighed. 'Yes, I see that I should have, but I did not for very good reasons. I thought that it would further complicate your difficult position.'

'Is he very angry?'

Jabir shook his head with a faint smile. 'Not really. It's more a case of pique than anything else.'

'Are you sure?' she asked anxiously. 'I would hate to be the cause of any trouble between you and your father.'

'It is nothing that I cannot handle. All will be well, Sara. Trust me.'

'Yes, I suppose I must,' she replied, trying hard to banish any thoughts about the unknown Nurra.

They sat in companionable silence. Jabir leaned back against the wall. 'Do you think you will like my children?' he asked.

'They're sweet! Honestly, when you said you wanted me to ... to be a mother to your little girls, I was absolutely terrified!' Sara smiled at Jabir across the bar. 'I mean, I've never had anything to do with small children. I thought you were out of your mind.'

'Maybe I was ... and am,' he said reflectively, staring into his glass.

'Well, I don't know whether I'm the right person for them, but I really will try and make them happy,' she assured him.

Jabir looked at the girl sitting opposite him, his eyes running over the gentle curve of her cheek, the soft fullness of her mouth.

'My dear Sara, I have every confidence that you will be like putty in their tiny hands, and will undoubtedly spoil them outrageously!' He laughed and leaned forward to pour them both another drink.

'What happened to their mother—your wife?' she asked, the question leaping unbidden to her lips.

There was a long silence as Jabir sat, very still, before slowly putting the bottle down on the bar. He gave a deep sigh. 'I don't want to talk about my first wife, Sara. Especially not here—not now. . . ' and he lapsed into a dark silence once more.

'I'm so sorry, I...' Sara was overcome by an extraordinary and overwhelming urge to hold and comfort the taut, unhappy figure in front of her.

He slowly lifted his head to look into her large blue eyes filled with distress. Suddenly his bleak features seemed to alter for a moment, his eyes gleamed and her heart began to thud and pound in her chest. The next instant his heavy eyelids descended to hide all expression in his face, and he got up, collecting their glasses and putting them in the small sink behind the bar.

'Come on, it's time we went in,' he said blandly. 'It has been a long day, and I for one feel like an early night.'

Their conversation was stilted as they walked back through the garden of the house, and as Sara glanced sideways at his hawk-like profile, she was filled with dismay. With just a few careless words she had managed to completely destroy what had been the delicate and tentative beginnings of a friendly relationship between herself and her new husband. How in the world could she have been so foolish?

CHAPTER FIVE

SARA awoke the next morning feeling very much as she had on going to sleep the night before—depressed.

Yashi knocked, and entered with an early morning cup of tea. She also brought with her a typewritten note from one of Jabir's staff informing her that her husband would be at the oil terminal all morning, but that she was expected to resume her Arabic tuition. Her tutor would await her pleasure in the library of the palace from nine till ten a.m.

'Oh, great!' she grumbled, and screwing up the note, threw it across the room in a brief fit of temper.

Taking her tea over to the open window, she tried hard to think about her situation with equanimity. It proved to be a hard task. Whatever sort of marriage she had been pressganged into, she simply had to try and make some sense of it.

Jabir had bought her, like someone might buy a loaf of bread. He had said he wanted her to be a hostess, but it had been quite plain, from her week on the yacht, that he had no such real need. All his problems seemed to be capable of being solved by a click of his arrogant fingers.

Besides, if he needed a hostess at any time, he could pick one of the glamorous women she had met at the party in Cannes. Any one of them wouldn't have hesitated to jump at the chance, she thought sourly.

Moreover, not only would they have been happy to serve as Jabir's hostesses, it had been quite clear to even her innocent eyes that some of the women would have been very happy—not to say eager—to have gone to bed with him as well. In fact, she was very sure that at least two of the women present, especially an Italian brunette with an amazing bosom, had done just that!

Despite her behaviour on their wedding night, and she blushed with mortification at how stupid she must have seemed, Sara wasn't entirely a fool. It was clear that Jabir found her attractive and wished to make love to her. Correction: she reminded herself bitterly, he wished to pursue 'a normal bodily function!' However, if he had wanted a mistress, there were obviously plenty of willing candidates available. He didn't have to marry her for that.

Mother for his children? It was possible, although in Scotty they already had a warm, surrogate mother. Besides, they were at school here, and Jabir had said he and Sara would be living mainly in the West.

So why, why, *why* had he married her? Thinking about John's words on the yacht gave her thoughts a new turn. Was it, somehow, to spite his father? The whole idea seemed ridiculous. Not only would it have been a stupid thing to do, and despite her mixed feelings about Jabir no one could ever call him stupid. He could easily have found someone else to fill the role. Buying her father's hotel was an expensive way to go about such a business.

Sara sipped her hot tea trying in vain to make some sort of sense out of her situation. There just was no rhyme or reason for her marriage, and at the thought of the long, lonely years in front of her a small tear trickled down her cheek.

Stop wallowing in self-pity, she told herself sternly. Jabir's children were the only possible if not particularly likely reason for her being in Assir, and at least she could concentrate on trying to make them happy. She got dressed quickly, and went along to the schoolroom where the children were finishing their breakfast.

She helped to get them ready for school, promising, at a request from Nadia, that she would take them swimming later in the afternoon. She was rewarded by a quick kiss and hug from the little girl, and took them down the stairs to where Hamid waited to escort them to their lessons.

'Poor wee mites, they need a mother's love,' said Scotty, standing beside her as they waved the children goodbye.

Sara hurried through breakfast, being served in solitary magnificence in the large empty dining room, and then, complying with Jabir's orders, made her way to the library for her Arabic lesson.

Her tutor, a dry wizened Arab who turned out to be the official librarian to the King, droned on about the various verb structures, until Sara had decided she'd had enough.

'Just a minute,' she said, cutting into his flow of words. 'All this is very necessary, but it's no use to me at the moment. I have to meet the King in about three hours' time, and what I need are a few polite phrases that I can learn and practise during the morning.'

'Certainly, Princess,' he had replied, and the lesson immediately took a more practical turn.

As her tutor left, Hassa bounced in bringing an invitation from her mother, the Queen, to call and have a cup of coffee, and Sara, grateful to escape from what she was fast beginning to think of as her prison, accepted with alacrity.

Hassa's mother received them in a beautiful room, with old paintings on the wall, and fragile china displayed on delicate French furniture. The Queen, a slim charming woman of about forty, sat dispensing coffee in delicate porcelain cups, and pressed Sara to some small biscuits.

'My dear, what wonderful hair!' she said in perfect English, with only a slight accent. 'And you're so lovely too. Jabir is a very lucky man.' Sara blushed. 'Has my daughter told you? We have arranged a luncheon party today for all the family.'

'Yes, Your—Your . . . um . . . Majesty.' Sara was in a quandary. Clearly, talking to royalty posed problems that she had not met before. What do I call the Queen? she thought in a panic. 'Yes, Hassa has told me it will be what she calls a "terrific do"!'

The Queen laughed. 'She would! Normally there are separate parties for women and men at the same time. But when it's just the family—as I told some of the King's old aunts—we really must move with the times. So it will be a thoroughly Western meal, and I hope you will feel at home.'

'Oh, I'm sure I shall. It's very kind of you.'

'Not at all.' The Queen paused, then said, 'My dear, titles are such a bore, and you are a member of our family now. Please won't you call me "Mother" like the rest of the children?'

'Thank you, I'd—I'd like that.' Sara smiled. 'Your daughter has been so kind and helpful to me.'

'So I should hope,' the Queen replied firmly. 'My goodness,' she added, 'it's just struck me how like Jabir's mother you are. It's quite a remarkable resemblance.'

'Jabir's mother?' said Hassa. 'That must have been ages ago.'

'Oh yes—I was quite young. Let's see, Jabir is thirty-two, so I must have been about ten or twelve at the time. However, I do remember just how lovely she was—quite exquisite. So tall and slender, with long blonde hair.' She turned to Sara. 'She was English, like you, my dear, and so sweet—everyone loved her. It was well known that the King adored the ground she walked on.'

'You never told me about this before,' said Hassa indignantly. 'How did my father meet her?'

'My dear, it all happened so long ago. Your father was in London for an Arab conference. She was the daughter of an English diplomat, and they met and fell in love. His father—the old King—was alive at the time, and there was a tremendous upset because your father was already married to a princess from Dubai— Muhammed's mother. However, your father divorced her—and they were married.'

'Oh! How romantic!' breathed Hassa.

'Yes, it was,' her mother smilingly agreed. 'They only

had a few years together, and then she died giving birth to Jabir. It was all very tragic. The King was inconsolable for a long time. He never talks about it ...'

'But, Mother, he's got you now.'

'Yes, of course,' the Queen smiled gently at her daughter. 'However, I suspect he still remembers her, as we all do.'

'... And then he married you,' prompted her daughter, 'and lived happily ever after!'

'Now, Hassa, that's quite enough! You've been encouraging me to gossip—what will Sara think of us?'

'I think ... I think that Hassa—and the King—are very lucky.' Sara smiled at the Queen. 'Thank you for telling me something of Jabir's background. It helps me to understand him better.'

After a few more minutes of general conversation, Hassa took Sara upstairs to see her wedding dress, and many of the presents which had already arrived for the wedding.

It was as she was leaving that the Queen suddenly exclaimed, 'How silly of me! If you want to know more about Jabir's mother, Sara, you should ask Miss Scott. When Queen Zahra came to Assir as a bride, she brought Miss Scott with her.'

'Queen Zahra? Her name was *Zahra*?' Sara looked with amazement at Hassa's mother.

'Yes,' the Queen smiled. 'You see why I was so surprised. Not only do you look like Jabir's mother, but the pronunciation of your name is the same. Extraordinary, is it not?'

'You're very honoured,' said Hassa as Sara took her leave. 'Hardly anyone gets to call her "Mother", and certainly not straight away.'

'I think she's so nice,' said Sara. 'I bet she makes your father very happy.'

'Yes, she does,' Hassa agreed. 'He hardly ever makes a move without her advice—which is why I'm quite sure he's going to approve of you. Don't be nervous of meeting him, Sara. He's a dear man really, he just gets on his high horse occasionally.'

'I'm trying not to feel too nervous,' said Sara, and glanced at her watch. 'I must go and change, though, or I really will be in disgrace.'

'I'll see you later,' said Hassa, giving her a kiss and waving her goodbye.

Later, as she stood surveying herself in the mirror, Sara was suddenly struck by doubts as to whether her dress was suitable for the reception, and hoping desperately that Jabir would return in time. The idea of attending such a party composed of all his relatives—completely on her own—was terrifying.

After much thought, she had decided to wear a simple, long, princess-line dress in a clear azure blue raw silk. Its high round neck was encrusted with rhinestones and pearls, as were the ends of the long sleeves, while her low-heeled court shoes had been dyed to match the colour of the dress. Her hair, freshly washed and dried, had been brushed off her face and then caught in a knot at the back of her head, where it flowed down to cover her shoulders.

You're not dressed in the first flush of fashion, she told herself wryly, thinking of the other women likely to be present, but at least she wasn't showing too much bare flesh, which should please the King.

'Perfect,' said a voice behind her, and she jumped with shock. Turning, she saw Jabir standing in the doorway which connected their two bedrooms. It was Jabir as she had never seen him before—in full Arabian dress. From the double gold cord on top of his white headdress, to his white under-robe and outer cloak, heavily trimmed with gold braid, he was the embodiment of all she had ever imagined a desert prince would be.

He stood, leaning against the door, with his arms folded, as he regarded her with a frown.

'What is this I hear?' he said sternly, and her heart sank. She tried desperately to think of what could have gone wrong. She must have done something . . .

'I've only been away for half a day, and yet I hear that the Palace is buzzing with the news that the Prince's new wife is as fair and lovely as the sun. I also hear,' his grim expression suddenly giving away to a wide smile, 'that she has charmed the King's wife, and is proving to be a kind and loving mother to her stepchildren!'

'Oh, Jabir! You liar!' she laughed with relief.

'My dear Sara, I have given you the expurgated version, I can assure you. The full flights of my countrymen's praise would indeed bring a blush to your cheeks, and since one of their favourite occupations is to gossip, your arrival has provided them with a feast. Don't worry—I'm delighted! My stock has risen enormously as a consequence.'

'How—how ridiculous . . .' she said, blushing.

'Yes, isn't it,' he agreed blandly. 'However, I'm sorry I had to be away on business. How is your Arabic tuition coming along?'

He looks . . . he looks absolutely fantastic, she thought in wonder, as he walked slowly towards her. His robes billowed about his tall figure as he moved, while his hooded eyes never left her face. Jabir's close proximity, as always, made her feel nervous, and she said breathlessly, 'Not—not very well, I'm afraid. Just a few words, like . . . er . . . *aghal* and *kaffiyeh*,' she said, indicating his headband and headcovering, '. . . and *aba*,' she put a hand on his cloak.

'Top of the class!' he said with a lazy smile, as he gazed down into her blue eyes. 'Now, how would you translate: I am going to kiss you, simply as a tribute to your beauty, and I do not—repeat not—intend to ravish your body . . .? For such a scholar of Arabic, that should not prove too difficult!'

Despite the wild beating of her heart, Sara couldn't suppress a small gurgle of laughter.

'Now, is that "yes", or is that "no"?' he asked quizzically.

She dropped her eyes, and trembled as he placed a

gentle hand under her chin, and slowly raised her blushing face towards him.

She gasped as his mouth touched a corner of hers. It was a gentle caress, a delicate pressure as his mouth explored the outline of her lips, softly and sensually. She felt a dizzy sense of imbalance and her hands groped blindly for support, as she felt her limbs trembling—weak with a longing she hardly understood.

Sara felt cruelly disappointed as Jabir carefully let her go, and she stood meekly acquiescent as he smoothed back a tendril of her hair.

'Perfect,' he said, and led her from the room.

She followed him through a side door into the King's Palace, and along a wide corridor past an army of servants who bowed as they passed. He came at last to a door covered in gold leaf and issued her through into a large, ornate and empty room.

'Is this where we meet the King?' she asked nervously.

'No, that's next door,' he said, and she was startled to see him remove his shoes and hand them to a servant waiting outside the door.

'It is the custom,' he said dismissively. 'Now, Sara,' he took her hands in his, 'I am now going to have a private word with my father in his study next door. You will wait here, and I will return to accompany you in to the main audience room. You understand?'

She nodded silently and he strode across the room and out through a small door in the far corner.

Left alone, Sara walked nervously around the room, before sitting down on one of the small red plush chairs set against the walls. Through the small door came the sound of a voice raised in anger, countered by the low tones of what she recognised as Jabir's voice. It went on for some time before there was a long pause, followed by a deep roll of laughter.

Some moments later the door opened, and Jabir returned. She looked anxiously at his face, as he gave her a brief reassuring smile and took her hand to lead her across to large double doors at the other side of the room, and into the *Majhis*, the King's audience chamber.

Sara looked across at the elderly, grey-haired man who sat on a raised dais leaning against a pile of silk cushions, as Jabir whispered to her to stand still until she was called. He walked forward a few paces, and knelt down, pressing his forehead to the Persian carpet on the marble floor. At a gesture from the King he rose and went forward, to kneel and kiss his father's hand.

Amazed at the deference her proud husband paid his father, Sara looked at the other men in Arab dress sitting around the room. They were all nodding with approval at Jabir's actions, so she concluded it must be the custom.

The King beckoned to Sara, who was momentarily shaken with nerves. However, she swiftly pulled herself together. Come on, she told herself. This is nothing but a tinpot desert kingdom, just remember you're British!

With a faint smile on her lips at such a ridiculously chauvinistic thought, and her head held high, Sara walked slowly forward down the length of the room, followed by a murmur of appreciation from the assembled company. She had no idea what to do, so she followed Jabir's lead, and knelt down before the King.

King Abdul spoke in Arabic, and Jabir translated: 'My father welcomes you to our house, and—prays that you will produce many grandsons for his old age.'

The embarrassing words confused Sara, who promptly forgot the carefully learnt Arabic phrases she had intended to say. The King spoke to Jabir, then turned towards her and, smiling, said a short sentence in Arabic. Sara couldn't, of course, understand a word of what he said, and in a blind panic she hesitated, then uttered one of the words racing around in her mind.

She was startled to see a broad smile break out on the King's face—and he threw back his head and roared with laughter. He stood up, and bent forward to help her to rise. He laughed again and kissed her forehead, before requesting her—in perfect English—to sit next to him.

Jabir sat down beside her, and she turned to him, as the King spoke in Arabic to his other guests.

'I'm sorry,' she whispered. 'I had a really good sentence all ready, and then I forgot it completely.'

'Don't worry. You passed with flying colours,' he chuckled. 'My father is just telling everyone else the joke against himself!'

'Jabir!' she hissed. *'What did I say?'*

'My father has a sense of humour. He knows very well that you are a Christian, and knowing equally well that you don't speak Arabic, he couldn't resist saying to you, "We hope you become a Moslem". You delighted him by coming straight back with the one and only perfect answer. You said, *"Insh'allah"*—If God wills it!'

A gale of laughter rang around the tent as the rest of the company enjoyed the joke against the King, who turned beaming at her, to pat her hand. He then turned and addressed his guests, in English. 'My son has chosen a beautiful and clever woman to be his wife. May he love and treasure her accordingly.' Sara sat blushing as the assembled guests cheered and clapped.

Jabir rose to his feet and replied in Arabic. Again the company laughed and applauded, with the addition of much winking and elbow nudging.

'What ... what did you just say?' she whispered, flushing slightly at the blatantly obvious glances of appreciation from some of the King's guests.

'It is ... er ... not translatable,' Jabir replied dismissively.

'I bet it's not!' she muttered in annoyance, looking around her at the all-male company. 'Well, maybe you can tell me who all these people are, and why there are no women present?'

'Some are old hunting friends of my father's. He is going off camping in the desert today, which is why this reception isn't being held tonight. Who else? Let's see ... there are some Government Ministers and a few of my uncles . . . As to the absence of women, it is not the custom. You are being honoured today, Sara.'

A few minutes later the King rose, and taking her hand suggested that they join the family. He led her into a room the size of a ballroom, filled with a chattering crowd.

She was greeted by the Queen and then, led by the King, who insisted on holding her hand, they moved slowly around greeting Jabir's relatives, one by one. Luckily, Hassa had told her the custom of women was for her to touch someone's fingertips and then raise her fingers to her lips. I won't have any lipstick left at this rate, she thought wryly.

She met aunts, uncles, cousins of the first degree, and not such important cousins of the third degree—it seemed to go on and on. Hassa came up, leading forward her husband-to-be, a shy good-looking young man, with a determined chin. He was telling her that he had just returned from an American university to work in one of the country's leading banks, when she saw a startlingly beautiful woman approach. Tall, slim and willowy, with black hair and gleaming magnolia skin, she wafted towards them, her flowing dress of scarlet and gold emphasising her fragile loveliness.

'I hope you are going to introduce me to your new wife, Jabir?' she said in a soft low musical voice.

Sara sensed a stiffening in Jabir and knew instinctively, before he performed the introductions, that this was Nurra, the widow of his dead brother, and the King's original choice for Jabir.

'My dear, what a surprise you gave us all!' cooed Nurra, flashing them both a dazzling smile which Sara noticed did not quite reach her glinting dark eyes. 'I must congratulate you, Jabir. Your wife is truly lovely, and I hope you will both be very happy.'

Sara's instinctive dislike for the beautiful Nurra was tempered by a grudging admiration of how the other woman was carrying off what could only have been, if

Hassa was to be believed, a potentially embarrassing situation.

Nurra's musical voice cut into her thoughts. 'Now, I know you two lovebirds will want to be together, *but I'm going to steal your husband, Sara*—just for a few minutes—of course!' Her rippling laugh grated on Sara's ears. 'It's old Uncle Sa'ad. He does so want to have a word with you, Jabir,' she confided, slipping an arm through his and leading him away into the crowd.

Well! She's certainly made her intentions perfectly clear. 'Steal my husband'—I can't say I haven't been warned, thought Sara with a spurt of anger, as she watched Nurra clinging to Jabir's arm, and looking up adoringly into his face.

Her thoughts were interrupted as lunch was announced and the King claimed her hand again, escorting her into another room. There, a low table almost as big as the room itself was groaning with large dishes piled high with food. The gold platters held young lamb on beds of rice, surrounded by bowls of bananas and peeled oranges, slices of lemon, boxes of Damascus sugared almonds, and much more.

Sara found herself placed between the King and Jabir, who she noticed had the beautiful Nurra on his other side. The King, clearly very taken with her, monopolised Sara throughout the meal, telling her tall stories of his old desert campaigns. Consequently she was unable to do more than glance sideways occasionally at Jabir and Nurra, who seemed to be enjoying themselves, chatting in Arabic to each other. Nurra's tinkling laugh was much in evidence as she frequently touched his arm.

The King was assiduous in his attentions to Sara, and insisted on pressing her to a titbit here and a delicious morsel there, until she had to refuse any more. 'I've never felt so full in all my life!' she laughed.

'You are a very beautiful woman,' he said, as they each washed their hands in the bowls of rosewater, drying their hands on damask napkins given to them by the servants. 'You remind me so much of my dear, dead wife, my beloved Zahra—Jabir's mother.' He sighed deeply. 'It was all so long ago, but yes, you are very like her—and your name is pronounced the same too—extraordinary!'

'But, Your Majesty, your present wife, Hassa's mother, is charming. She has been so kind to me.'

The King smiled. 'Yes, she told me I should love you—as indeed I do. She is a very clever woman.'

The servants brought in the incense and as its pungent fragrance filled the room, the King stood up indicating that the luncheon party was over. He kissed Sara on the cheek, bidding her a fond farewell.

'My son,' he said to Jabir, 'you must join me in the desert soon, and bring your lovely wife.'

As they turned to go, Sara was pleased to see the look of dark fury that crossed Nurra's face at the King's invitation.

Having made their farewells, Jabir and Sara walked back to their house; she to change and take the little girls swimming as promised, while Jabir had yet another business meeting.

They entered the hall, and as they began to mount the stairs he said, 'My father tells me that he finds you enchanting, and thoroughly approves of my choice of wife. I—I am very pleased that he should think so. I was also very pleased and very proud of you today, Sara.'

She blushed with pleasure at his words. 'He was very sweet and kind to me. All your family were. I must say,' she added, 'I liked Hassa's fiancé, he's obviously very clever.'

'He'll need to be!' Jabir laughed. 'Hassa will run rings around him if he does't watch out, just as Nurra was far too headstrong for my brother.'

'Whereas, at the snap of *your* fingers, she would be as good as gold, I suppose?' Sara said waspishly.

'Oh yes,' said Jabir with a faint smile. 'I don't usually have any trouble with women.'

'I bet you don't!' Sara was incensed at his arrogant male complacency. 'Especially with a dark, flashy number like Nurra!' she snapped, before running into her bedroom and slamming the door behind her.

Sara was somewhat apprehensive and bitterly regretted her outburst earlier in the day. She therefore took particular pains to look as attractive as possible as she dressed for dinner that night. She felt ashamed to have shown such a petty jealousy of Nurra, and hoped that Jabir would have forgotten the incident.

As she tied the thin shoulder straps of her simple cream chiffon dress, she tried to banish the image of Nurra and Jabir together, concentrating instead on brushing her hair so that it fell in a long stream over her bare shoulders, which rose from the tight bodice moulded to her figure. The finely pleated skirt swayed about her slim legs as she left the room and walked downstairs.

Jabir appeared to be in an unusually good mood as he told her about his uncle Sa'ad who bred Salukis, the hunting dogs of the Bedouin. Jabir and Sara were to be given two puppies as a wedding present.

Sitting over dinner as he described how the dogs were used for hunting, she thought that, as usual, he looked superb. His thin white silk shirt was unbuttoned far enough to display his gold chain and medallion nestling in the dark hairs of his broad chest. A wide black belt with a large flat gold buckle clasped his slim waist, below which he wore a pair of well cut dark trousers.

No wonder he never has any trouble with women, she thought wryly, as they returned to the drawing room for coffee. He's sensationally attractive—and he knows it!

'Now, Sara!' he said, as they sipped their coffee, 'since we are agreed that your dossier is totally inadequate, you must tell me what you like to do in your spare time.'

'Spare time? You do remember the hotel, Jabir?' she

smiled faintly. 'How much spare time do you think I had?'

'Yes, I understand how it must have been, but given a choice do you like to read books or listen to music?'

'I like to read when I can. I'm very fond of whodunits and ghost stories. When I was younger, I used to frighten myself to death, and then couldn't sleep at night!'

'And music? Dancing?' he queried.

'I think you got taken for a ride by your investigators. I should ask for your money back!' She grinned at him, her lovely blue eyes twinkling. 'Yes, I like music of all kinds, and I must say,' she added wistfully, 'I did love going to discos when I had the chance. Which wasn't very often.'

'My dear wife, that is a matter which is easily remedied,' he said, getting up and going over to a switch box by the large window. He opened the box and pushed a button.

The result of his simple action was startling. The lights dimmed, soft music filled the air, and small spotlights in different colours began to revolve in each corner of the room.

Sara stood up, her mouth open in astonishment. 'For heaven's sake,' she said at last. 'What a fantastic set-up!'

Jabir strolled over to her side. 'The mad architect again! I'm afraid I haven't appreciated his genius, until now. May I have the pleasure?' he added.

'What?' She turned, startled.

'My dear Sara, you said you liked dancing—therefore let us dance,' he said gently, taking her into his arms. She found the close contact with his body made her stomach knot with tension, and she nervously held herself stiffly away from him as they moved over the marble floor.

'Sara,' Jabir bent his head to whisper in her ear, 'this is not the Military Two-Step, and we are married! Do you think,' he laughed softly, 'that you could possibly relax?'

He felt her surprised gurgle of laughter. 'That's better,' he said. 'Now put your arms around my neck. I promise you, you'll be quite safe—I don't bite!'

Thankful for the dim light which hid her blushes, Sara slowly did as she was bid—not feeling at all safe. In fact she felt nervous tremors of excitement run through her frame as he placed his cool cheek next to hers and drew her soft figure against his hard body, placing his hands lightly but firmly about her.

They slowly swayed to the music and her heart began to thud as he drew her closer and closer to him. Nervous ripples of excitement gradually shook her body, as his arms tightened about her, and he slowly trailed his lips over her forehead to her temples, and down her cheek.

Helpless to control the rising tide of desire which coursed through her trembling body, she gasped as his mouth touched a corner of her lips.

Slowly, tantalisingly, Jabir explored her soft mouth with small gentle kisses, before his warm firm lips gradually became more insistent. Sara felt as though she was drowning as his kiss deepened, and he forced her lips apart, sensuously exploring the inner softness of her mouth.

He placed his long slim hands either side of her head, and slowly withdrawing his mouth, looked down at her in the dim light: at the trembling temptation of her lips and her fluttering eyelids as she gazed sightlessly back at him, totally in the thrall of a tide of passionate desire.

'Oh, Sara!' he groaned softly, and buried his face in her soft hair, folding her within his arms and holding her tightly as he would a child, until the taped music ended.

It took them both some time to realise exactly where they were. She glanced up at his pale, stern face. He looks as shattered as I feel, was her first coherent thought, as he slowly let her go and walking to the drinks cupboard, returned to silently hand her a glass.

As she sipped the cool liquid, reality returned with a vengeance. A deep blush spread across her features, as she recalled how her body had betrayed her, and totally unable to say anything, she buried her nose in the drink to hide her confusion.

Jabir, looking at her intently, cleared his throat. He was clearly about to speak, when the telephone in the corner gave an abrupt ring. Cursing under his breath, he went over and lifted the receiver.

'Yes, that's all right. Yes, I understand. Tomorrow?' There was a pause, followed by his sigh. 'Very well, I'll be over in a minute.' He put down the receiver.

'I have to go out,' he said harshly. 'I . . .'

'That's all right, Jabir.' Sara put down her glass on the table, moving over to the door. 'It's very late and I'm—I'm very tired,' she said in a small, thin voice.

'Sara,' he breathed, 'don't go. I . . .'

'Goodnight, Jabir,' she said as firmly as she could, before slipping silently away.

She sat by her open window, hoping that the night breeze from the sea would cool her heated body. Jabir's experienced lovemaking had roused her senses to such a pitch that every nerve end of her being cried out for sexual satisfaction.

The room was a dark cavern behind her as she looked over the gardens of the Palace complex. The trees were lit by spotlights which outlined the delicate tracery of their branches, while the moon turned their leaves to silver.

In the still night, she heard a door open and then bang shut, followed by footsteps coming from the house opposite. Idly she looked down and then stiffened, her eyes wide with shock, as Jabir came into view. She watched his figure as he crossed the lawn and disappeared into the house. Hardly daring to breathe, she heard him mount the stairs and hesitate outside her room, before continuing along to his suite.

Still in shock, she looked over at the house opposite—Nurra's house! He couldn't ... Not Nurra ... He wouldn't! Her stomach knotted with such a surge of jealousy that she felt sick. Oh yes, he could— and would—a small voice said inside her. He's quite capable and ruthless enough to do anything!

Stumbling over to her bed, she threw herself across it, her body racked with pain as she tormented herself imagining Jabir's lovemaking with the beautiful Nurra. Her pillow was wet with helpless tears by the time she eventually fell into an exhausted sleep, as the faint glow of dawn lit the sky.

CHAPTER SIX

SARA sat in one of the little enclosed courtyards which were to be found in the grounds of Jabir's house. The brown sandstone walls were covered in some exotic flowering vine, whose long tendrils hung down, gently waving in the breeze from the sea. The flooring of green malachite surrounded the pale green alabaster fountain, the spray of which rose to fall in a myriad tiny glistening droplets on to the pink waterlilies which filled the small pool. The air was heavy with perfume from the creamy white flowers which grew in profusion around the small enclosure.

From the canopied shade of her reclining chair, Sara viewed the enchanting scene before her with dull, unseeing eyes. She had, not surprisingly, overslept that morning, and had only woken when her maid Yashi had brought in her breakfast tray. Ignoring the rolls and coffee, Sara had stumbled into her bathroom, and had stood under the shower, which had helped to wake her up, if not to revive her spirits.

Dressing simply in a pink sleeveless dress, she had ignored her breakfast, and grabbing her sunglasses had left her room to go downstairs—desperate to get out of the house, and into the fresh air.

About to descend the stairs, she noticed that the door to Jabir's suite was ajar. Almost without conscious thought she moved slowly along the upper landing, and stood in the open doorway. His sitting-room was severely masculine, containing black leather chairs, deep glowing Persian carpets on the marble floor, and a large ornate desk inlaid with brass and tortoiseshell, edged with ormolu mounts. One wall was lined with books, and the others held large gilt-framed oil paintings, set above slim cabinets of the same brass and tortoiseshell as the desk.

Sara knew nothing about art, but even her uncritical eyes could tell that these pictures, mainly of horses, were something quite out of the ordinary. She walked slowly over to read a small brass plate on the bottom of one of the frames: 'Mare and Foal—George Stubbs'. She looked at the peaceful scene set in a wooded landscape, for some time, then turned to survey the rest of the room. No books were open on the tables, no personal clutter on the empty desk—everything spoke of order and method. If rooms were said to embody people's personality, Jabir's sitting room seemed a fair indication of his character as she knew it; dark, sombre and magnificently austere.

She had shivered suddenly, and run from the room, down the stairs and out into the Palace grounds, where, wandering aimlessly, she had come upon this peaceful courtyard.

She heard a step and looked up. Yashi was regarding her anxiously, and putting down a tray on the low table in front of Sara, said, 'You no eat. Must have coffee.'

'Thank you, Yashi,' said Sara, trying to smile at the maid, who disappeared as quickly as she had come.

Sighing deeply, Sara poured herself a cup of coffee and leant back in her chair. The fresh morning air and her peaceful surroundings should have been balm to her troubled spirits. Certainly, the cold light of day brought with it a more reasoning frame of mind than the fevered fantasies of the night before.

However, the end result was the same. It seemed as if her husband had been, and was continuing to have, an affair with Nurra, despite the fact that he had only just married Sara. Why, if he wanted Nurra so much, hadn't he married her in the first place as his father wanted?

Nevertheless Jabir, she told herself, might be many things, but he certainly wasn't a fool. He, a recently married man, was committing adultery, and even Sara knew of the extreme penalties for such action in Moslem countries. If the death penalty was no longer on the statute books in this day and age, adultery was still regarded as one of the more heinous crimes.

A tiny flame of optimism suddenly flowed within her tired brain. Maybe it was all a mistake, and he had been at another house last night—not Nurra's? But her next thought brought her hopes crashing down again. She was living in Assir, a desert kingdom whose ancient laws were more concerned with keeping women under control than disciplining men who could apparently have four wives at any one time. In such a masculine-orientated society, Jabir was undoubtedly quite safe.

Whatever there was between Jabir and Nurra, it paled into insignificance beside the one traumatic and disastrously obvious conclusion to be drawn from her unhappy and sleepless night.

Somehow, and at some point, between their first meeting in the hotel and that—that dance last night, Jabir had in those few short weeks not just bought himself a wife, *but had taken possession of her heart as well!*

How could she have been so stupid? she railed at herself. Maybe if she had been more experienced, indulged in affairs like some of her friends, she might have recognised what was happening to her. She would have realised why she was always so breathless and nervous in his company—why one glance from his eyes made her feel weak and trembling. What a fool she was! There must be a way to stop oneself falling in love, she told herself miserably. Even now it might not be too late. Perhaps if she managed to steel herself against Jabir, indifference would come in time.

Sara sighed, as she made her brave resolutions. She knew it was no use. Her newly heightened emotions told her it was a waste of time. Already, as she was talking so bravely to herself, she felt a desperate longing once more to have Jabir's mouth pressed closely to hers, and to feel his arms around her.

His experienced lovemaking had aroused her dormant passions to a pitch where they cried out for satisfaction.

She realised that, given her wedding night back again, she would not repulse Jabir—she wanted to surrender to him, completely and entirely.

She flushed with shame at her thoughts. Not because there was anything shameful in her tortured feelings, but because there was no way in which they could ever be reciprocated. She was in love with her husband, who made it quite clear—as clear as daylight—*that he didn't love her*!

Oh yes, he found her attractive and could, and undoubtedly would, make love to her; but only from the physical desire to possess a beautiful woman—what he called a 'normal bodily function'.

Tears of self-pity and tiredness from her sleepless night filled her eyes. She had to blow her nose very hard and drink another cup of coffee, before she managed to pull herself together. She put on her dark glasses to hide her puffy eyes, and lay back exhausted in her chair.

The soft sea breeze ruffled the vine, and as the bees hummed amongst the flowers, she closed her eyes to savour their languorous perfume which filled the courtyard ...

The next thing she knew was that she heard a small, delicate cough. Startled, she opened her eyes to see Nurra standing in front of her.

'Nurra, I'm sorry—I must have been dozing in the sun ...' Sara sat up, startled. What on earth is she doing here? she thought, bemused and still half asleep.

'Sara—please! I didn't realise you were resting. I'll go away if you like?' Nurra's musical voice was low, and not unfriendly.

'No, of course not. Won't you sit down and join me for some coffee?'

Sara sighed inwardly. What else could she do? She couldn't just tell the woman to go away, however much she wanted to. Nurra was looking ravishingly pretty in a cool white linen dress with a scarlet belt and matching red high-heeled sandals. Her black hair was piled up on top of her head, emphasising her delicate swan-like neck, and Sara felt herself sinking into a sea of despair. How could anyone, let alone Jabir, resist this woman's startling beauty and sophistication?

'Coffee? Well,' Nurra laughed, 'when I heard where you were, I did ask your maid to bring us a fresh pot. You don't mind?'

'I think it's an excellent idea,' said Sara decisively. The strong coffee would do her good, and any conversation, even with Nurra, was marginally better than having to listen to her own miserable thoughts.

Yashi brought a fresh tray, and as Nurra took her cup she smiled at Sara. 'I had to come over and see you. I knew Hassa was spending the day with her future mother-in-law, and wouldn't be able to tell you what a great success you were yesterday.'

Sara looked at her, startled. 'Oh no, I'm sure ... everyone has been so kind ...'

'No, really.' Nurra smiled brilliantly at Sara. 'The family were enchanted with Jabir's new wife, which is why I thought I really must come over and talk to you.'

It's her smile, thought Sara from behind the safety of her dark glasses. It's that ghastly smile which never quite reaches her hard eyes. That's definitely one of the things that I particularly dislike about Nurra.

'I thought we all got through that lunch yesterday rather well, don't you? Of course, everyone knew that the King wished Jabir to marry me,' Nurra continued, with a glint in her eyes, 'and it could have been very awkward for both of us.'

Sara murmured noncommittally.

'Frankly, Sara, I wasn't feeling too well disposed towards you. No one, and certainly not I, likes to be made to look a fool!' Nurra's voice, normally quiet and low, became taut and hard. She quickly recovered herself, and took a sip of coffee.

'However,' she continued, 'it's all that silly old man's fault, and I don't see why you and I should have to go around pretending that nothing has happened, and trying to avoid each other's company. The fastest way for all this business to die down is for us to at least appear to be friendly. That will stop any stupid gossip straight away.'

Sara, rather shocked at Nurra's ·reference to the King as a 'silly old man' nevertheless had to admit the sense of what Nurra had said. Whatever the situation there was nothing to be gained by causing talk in the claustrophobic family atmosphere of the Palace.

'Yes,' she said flatly, 'I take your point, Nurra.'

'It all comes down to family politics and the role of women in this country.' Nurra's face darkened with anger. 'As soon as my husband died, I wasn't just a widow—oh no! I was a bargaining counter. The King needs to keep my father's support, so he hunted around for someone else in his family to marry me.' She clenched her teeth in rage.

'You wouldn't believe it, Sara—he even considered old Uncle Sa'ad! The old boy is sixty-nine if he's a day, and lives with his home crammed full of dogs—ugh! You really can't blame me for my relief when the King finally decided upon Jabir. I mean, which would you have preferred?' She gave a harsh laugh, and even Sara had to smile briefly.

'Surely you had some say in the matter?' she asked.

'No, not really. When my husband died, I didn't want to marry anyone. But life for a woman alone in this country is not easy. All my family are in the north, so where could I go, and what would I do?

'Mind you,' Nurra said slowly, 'Jabir is very attractive and was certainly my best available choice, but I really wasn't too happy about it. Not after what happened to his first marriage.'

'His first marriage?'

'Well, I expect you know all about that?' said Nurra, with a swift look at the blonde girl beside her.

'No, I—Jabir doesn't like to talk about it,' Sara confided, with a rush. It seemed as if Nurra wasn't the 'other woman'—well, not in the usual sense anyway, and Sara was consumed by an overwhelming need to know about the woman her husband had married.

'Hasn't Hassa said anything? I've never known that silly little girl to keep her mouth shut for five minutes!' Nurra said spitefully.

'No, she said she couldn't.' Sara sprang to the defence of her new sister-in-law. 'Jabir had asked her not to talk about it, so she didn't. I—I simply can't understand why there's this silence.'

Sara felt a qualm at being so disloyal to Jabir, but the urge to satisfy her curiosity was irresistible.

'Well, well!' said Nurra, lapsing into a thoughtful silence as she slowly drank her coffee.

'Did you know Jabir's wife?' Sara prompted.

Nurra gave a bitter laugh. 'Oh yes—she was my sister!'

'Your sister? Nurra, I had no idea! I'm so sorry, I wouldn't have said anything if I'd known.' Sara looked at the woman in sympathy.

'Please, Sara, there's no need to worry. It's a relief to be able to talk about her. You see, our mother died when we were young, and my father married again. Miriam was younger than me, and—well, we were everything to one another. It—it all seemed so wonderful when our father told us that we were to marry the King's sons. We would be able to be together—always. Our family is a very old one. My ancestors used to be kings of this land, when the present Royal Family were just humble Bedouin,' her voice rang out proudly. 'We liked the Princes, and so it was all arranged.'

Sara remained silent, as Nurra continued, 'Miriam was so beautiful, you can have no idea of how lovely she was.' Her cat-like eyes flicked sideways at Sara, her voice losing its stridency and becoming low and musical, as she talked about her sister. 'Miriam and Jabir were so in love. They were so happy, so content. They had little Nadia, who was such a sweet baby, and then . . .'

'Then?' breathed Sara.

'Then the King sent Jabir abroad permanently on business and Miriam hardly ever saw him again. I don't suppose one can blame Jabir—enjoying the Western way of life, and the women, of course—but Miriam was so lonely, so unhappy . . .' Her voice fell.

'Miriam went home to our father for a long visit, and—it was so tragic—she was out for a drive in her car one day, and had a head-on collision with a bus. She died instantly.'

'How awful!' Sara sighed.

'Jabir was shattered, as you can imagine. He never forgave himself, you see. Oh yes,' Nurra's feline eyes fixed themselves firmly on Sara, 'he realised too late, far too late, how much he had loved his wife.'

Her low voice took on an almost hypnotic quality, as she continued softly, 'He had loved her before, of course, but now he loved her more than ever. Far, far more.' The words seemed to echo and tremble in the air as Sara, unable to move, was caught up in the atmosphere of the moment, staring mesmerised at Nurra.

'Oh yes,' crooned Nurra. 'He discovered that love such as theirs can never die. Miriam still lives—she lives in Jabir's heart.

'And so you see,' she added, the words falling like clear smooth pebbles into a crystal pool, 'and so you see why it was only for reasons of state that I agreed to marry Jabir. You and I, Sara, we are flesh and blood. How could we hope to compare or compete with a ghost? Miriam will never grow old, as we shall. She will remain fresh and lovely for all time, locked in Jabir's heart for ever.'

Nurra fell silent as Sara, the blood draining from her face, felt her heart slowly crack, and shatter into a myriad tiny pieces. The pause lengthened and Sara, who like Pandora had opened a forbidden box, now surveyed its contents with horrified dismay.

The pause lengthened, to be rudely shattered by the entrance of Yashi.

'Princess—your lesson. Your teacher awaits.'

'Yes, of course.' Sara's body seemed suddenly very heavy as she rose from her chair. She turned to Nurra. 'I'm sorry, it's my Arabic lesson—I must go.'

Nurra looked up at Sara. 'Maybe ... maybe I shouldn't have said anything, but it seemed wrong that you should not know the truth.'

Sara could only nod dumbly, not able to trust herself to speak, as she turned and left the courtyard on leaden feet.

Left alone, Nurra sat quietly for a moment, then rose in a slow, fluid motion, walking over to the alabaster fountain. She put out a hand to catch some of the fine spray from the cascading water, and then, with a small smile of satisfaction on her lips, walked slowly out of the courtyard.

How Sara staggered through her Arabic lesson and lunch with the children, she never knew. Miss Scott regarded her with concern. 'You don't look at all well, dear. It's maybe the heat. Why don't you go and lie down, and have a wee rest?'

Later, in her room, with the curtains drawn against the intense afternoon sun, Sara gave way to despair. There had been the faint possibility, hardly acknowledged to herself this morning, that maybe ... maybe Jabir would in time come to love her as she loved him. She now surveyed the cold ashes of such a hopeless desire.

How could she possibly compete against a dead woman, whose fresh and lovely face was always vibrantly alive for her husband? Nurra had provided the answer to much that had puzzled Sara. Her sister was locked in Jabir's heart, and there was no room for anyone else. His love was still so strong that he obviously couldn't bear to have her name mentioned— *for Jabir, Miriam lived*!

Sara wept hopelessly. There was nothing she could do—nothing. She was as firmly trapped by her love for Jabir as he was by his love for the dead Miriam.

She sat up in bed, with her arms around her drawn-up knees, rocking herself back and forth as desperate sobs shook her slim body. God, what a mess!

She crawled slowly out of bed and went to wash her face in cold water. Glancing at the mirror, she was appalled to see her pale reflection dominated by the deep shadows under her blue eyes, still glistening with tears. You must pull yourself together, she said desperately to herself in the mirror. You can't let anyone see you like this, especially not Jabir!

Sitting in front of her dressing-table, trying to camouflage her face with make-up, she suddenly remembered something that her father's girl-friend, Ann, had said in London. 'Why not try and concentrate on the children?' Sara sighed. Why not, indeed? They were lonely little girls, as much in need of love as she was. Perhaps she could give them all the love and devotion that was quite clearly not wanted, or needed, by Jabir. With firm resolution she looked at her watch. It was almost bedtime for the children—she would go and help Miss Scott with their bath and read them a story.

Miss Scott was happy to accept Sara's offer of help. 'You can give them their bath, dear, if you like. Just watch out for that Nadia, ooh—she's a naughty one!'

Despite her traumatic day, Sara found considerable comfort and balm for her ever-present misery in helping the little girls to undress and get into the bath. Mara, aged five, was still shy, but even her reserve broke down as Sara scrubbed and tickled her tummy.

Her back was turned as she carefully washed Mara's face, when she suddenly felt a swoosh of water over her head. Nadia, aged seven, and as naughty as Miss Scott had predicted she would be, was scooping up her bathwater with a toothmug and directing it in Sara's direction.

'Oh, Nadia, you wretch!' Sara laughed. 'You can jolly well have some of your own medicine!' and flicked a handful of water back at the little girl.

Mara climbed out of the bath and was jumping up and down excitedly, as battle was fairly joined. Nadia managed to strike home with a huge wave of water straight into Sara's face. Laughing hysterically, she began to grope blindly for a towel to wipe her sopping wet face and hair.

'I think this is what you are looking for,' said an amused voice, and still laughing, she threw back her long wet hair, to find her husband standing inside the doorway of the bathroom, with a towel in his outstretched hand.

The laugh died on her lips and her heart started to pound as she looked at Jabir. He had obviously just had a shower and changed, as his damp hair testified. The strong column of his throat rose from the open collar of his pale shirt, which was tightly stretched over his broad shoulders. His sleeves were rolled up above his strong muscular arms, and his cream trousers enclosed his slim hips like a second skin.

She felt quite dizzy as he took her hand and said with his lazy smile, 'There's no need to look so worried, Sara. My children seem to be enjoying themselves.'

'Daddy, Daddy!' the children chorused, as they flung themselves at their father.

'Get yourselves dry first,' he commanded with mock seriousness. 'You won't catch me getting wet like Sara. She was quite right, Nadia—you are a wretch! Now, I will come and read you a story in ten minutes, so you had better be dry, dressed and in bed!' and laughing he left the room.

Jabir was watching us all the time, thought Sara in dismay, as she dried and powdered the girls. He must think I'm very silly and juvenile. She helped the children to put on their nighties, gave them each a kiss and sent them, looking angelic, along to their father.

Since Jabir had decided to dress casually for dinner that night, Sara chose a simple black wrap-around dress, with a deep V-neck which fastened with two buttons at the waist. Her hair, still damp, hung loosely

down her back as, with as much resolution as she could
muster, she went downstairs.

Jabir was in the drawing room by the drinks cabinet,
pouring some champagne. He very rarely drank, in
deference to his Moslem faith, but when he did it was
always champagne.

If only dear old Dad could see me now! thought
Sara, smiling wryly. A princess, with an army of
servants to administer to her every whim, and
drinking champagne before dinner. It all sounds so
wonderful, and yet, without Jabir's love, and knowing
how he feels about his dead wife, it's nothing but
wormwood and gall.

'You look as though something has amused you,
Sara?' said Jabir, handing her a glass.

'No—quite the reverse,' she said shortly, burying her
nose in the rising bubbles of her drink.

There was a pause while Jabir walked over to sit
down in an easy chair. 'I have managed to sort out my
business affairs, and have decided that we will spend a
few days in the desert. I suggest, therefore, that we leave
tomorrow morning. These arrangements will suit you,
Sara?'

As if I had any say in the matter, she thought
sullenly, then immediately cheered up at the thought of
leaving the Palace complex. Being able to get away
from Nurra, and all she represented, would be
wonderful.

'It sounds a lovely idea, Jabir. Is it ... er ... very
primitive in the desert?' she asked. 'I mean—I'm sorry
to ask such a feminine question—but what do I wear?'

'I wouldn't say it was exactly "primitive",' his lips
twitched. 'It all depends what you mean. You can wear
trousers for the journey, if you like, which will be by
Land Rover, otherwise your normal clothes will be
perfectly acceptable.'

He looked at Sara, sitting on the arm of a chair, her
body turned slightly towards him. The black dress set
off her blonde hair and slight tan to perfection, while

the tight cross-over bodice of her dress emphasised the swelling shape of her full breasts.

She caught the dark gleam in his eyes as they roamed over her figure, and remembering their dance of last night, she began to feel the nervous tension rising in her stomach. She struggled not to blush, and to keep her face as impassive as his own.

He got up to fill her glass again, and said, 'I have been at fault.' Sara looked at him, her eyes widening with surprise, as he returned to his seat. 'I have failed to tell you how pleased I am that you are becoming such friends with my children. If you can make them happy, you will earn my deep gratitude.'

Gratitude be damned! she thought with a sudden flash of anger at her predicament, when all I want is your love. Struck by a thought, she hesitated and then plunged in. 'Jabir, do you think we could . . . could take your children with us tomorrow? I mean, it sounds just the sort of adventure I would have loved at their age. Please?'

Jabir looked into her pleading eyes and smiled regretfully. 'I'm sorry, Sara. I have plans for our trip to the desert, and they do not include the children, I'm afraid. However, it is a kind thought of yours, and we will take them soon, I promise. At the same time,' he added with a laugh, 'I will insist on taking Scotty—we can't have you wringing wet again!'

Sara flushed with embarrassment at the figure she must have looked in the bathroom. Just like a drowned rat, she thought in dismay.

Correctly interpreting her thoughts as usual, Jabir raised his hands. 'Please, Sara, it was . . .' He hesitated. 'I have lived in this house for seven years,' he said slowly, 'and tonight was the first time that I have heard genuine, joyous laughter echoing in the corridors. Every home should be full of laughter, don't you think?'

He stood up, and said, 'Come, we must eat. I have, alas, a meeting with the Minister for Foreign Development, so I will have to leave after dinner.' He walked over and took her hand, raising it to his firm lips, before ushering her from the room.

As she slowly undressed later that night, Sara was puzzled and disturbed. How could there have been no laughter in the house for the last seven years? Hassa had told her that Jabir had lived there since just before Nadia's birth. He had been so happy with his wife— how could there have been no laughter?

Sara climbed into bed, still so emotionally wrought up that she was unable to sleep. After tossing and turning for a bit, she gave up the unequal struggle, and decided to read a book instead.

She had been reading for about half an hour when there was a knock at the door which communicated with Jabir's suite. She looked up startled as her husband entered the room.

'My meeting finished early,' he said. 'May I come and talk to you for a minute or two, Sara?'

She blushed and nodded, looking down blindly at her book.

Jabir walked over to stand by the bed, looking down at his wife's bowed head. 'I—er—think you would find it easier to read it the other way up,' he said in an amused voice, picking up the book and placing it on her bedside table. 'I just want to talk to you, Sara. It's all right—I won't eat you!'

It's his other appetite that worries me, she thought in confusion, as he sat down on the bed and took her hands in his. She glanced nervously at him, her heart pounding at his proximity while the gleam in his eyes as they rested on her breasts rising and falling beneath the thin white silk nightgown caused her to tremble.

'It's all right, Sara, you can calm down. I want to talk to you. That's all I intend to do—at the moment. All right?'

'Yes,' she whispered.

'First of all, I can understand that the first night of our marriage was a considerable shock to you. We both blundered into a crevasse there, didn't we? I, because I had naturally assumed one thing, and you—well, you hadn't assumed anything at all. Yes?'

Sara nodded her head.

'Now, Sara,' he said quietly, 'I must tell you plainly that I know quite a lot about women. I was married for some years, and after that—well . . .'

'You mean you've had a lot of affairs?' she said, raising her eyes to his face.

'Yes,' he answered, looking gently down at her. 'It's not something I'm particularly proud of—but yes. So I would like you to accept the fact that I am fairly experienced, as far as knowing when a man and a woman are attracted to each other.'

'But that's just . . .!'

'Hush—let me finish,' he said. 'Now, I know that I find you very lovely, very sexually attractive, and that I desire to possess your body. That, you will say, sounds cold-blooded, but I can assure you, my dear Sara, that I am not.'

He moved to lean sideways across her body, while with a hand he gently brushed the hair from her brow.

'I desire you,' he said, his voice thickening, 'with all the passion a man can feel for a woman. But—and it's a big "but",' he added, running his hand down her soft cheek, 'you shy away like a startled filly whenever I come near you.'

The warmth of his fingers as they slipped down her neck and began to stroke her slim shoulder caused tremors of excitement to dance across her skin as Jabir continued. 'And yet . . . and yet whenever I have kissed or embraced you, you have responded quite differently! I am very certain that whether you know it or not—and I suspect that you do know it—you are now very much aware of me in the physical sense. That, in fact, you want me as much as I want you. Even if you won't admit it, your kisses and your body betray you every time.'

'No, Jabir, you don't understand . . .' Sara began to tremble again, as his hand moved slowly downwards to caress her breast, its rosy tip hardening under his fingers.

'Oh yes, I do understand. Whatever your mind may be saying, and despite any protestations you may make to me, your body is telling me something quite different. You, my darling Sara, give every promise of being a deeply passionate woman!'

'No! Please, no . . .' she whispered desperately. Jabir was right, she did understand—only too well! A few more minutes of his experienced caressing touch, and she would forget Miriam—forget everything—utterly powerless to resist the overwhelming urge to give herself freely to him, as her love demanded.

He gently withdrew his hand, and bent forward to give her a brief kiss on her cheek. 'It is important that you become aware—and honest—about your own physical needs, my Sara, or you will cause yourself, and me, much distress and unhappiness. Go to sleep now, we have a long journey ahead of us tomorrow. But please think about what I have said. Yes?'

She could only nod silently as he stood up and walked over to the door, letting it close with a click behind him.

The traumatic events of the day finally caught up with Sara, and she felt unable to think about anything—anything except Jabir. Her trembling body cried out for his touch, and it was some considerable time before she managed to fall into an exhausted sleep.

CHAPTER SEVEN

THE huge eight-gear, long-wheel-base Land Rover ground through the desert track, in the late afternoon sun. Sara turned to look out through the rear window, to make sure the rest of the cavalcade were still with them. Hamid waved from the Land Rover behind, which Jabir said contained food and equipment.

'The air smells so wonderful, Jabir—so fresh!' She felt exhilarated at having left behind the hothouse atmosphere at the Palace, and glanced over at her husband, his strong arms turning the wheel this way and that, as he dealt with the desert terrain. He felt her glance, and turned to smile before concentrating once more on the route ahead.

He was dressed in a fawn safari suit, with short sleeves, and he wore a red and white *kaffiyah*, held down on his head by a black-roped *aghal*. He looks magnificently at home in the desert, she thought, his broad shoulders touching her own for a moment, as he made a sudden turn of the wheel.

Sara leaned back in her seat, grateful for the sunglasses which hid her eyes. She had to be so careful when she was in Jabir's company. He had said her face was expressive, but there were times that she suspected him of clairvoyance. His ability to read her mind was uncanny, and it would require all her concentration, when in his presence, not to give away the secret of her love for him.

It was all she had—her pride and self-respect. It would be so easy to let Jabir know she welcomed his advances, especially after his talk to her last night. Her face flushed, as she was unable to control a sudden and urgent surge of desire for his touch.

A few minutes later she had herself in hand. Suppose

they did make love—what then? How long could she
hope to disguise from Jabir exactly how she felt about
him? She could imagine the embarrassment he would
feel, and her consequent feelings of shame and disgust.
Pride might be a sin, but she was nevertheless far too
proud to contemplate the thought of Jabir feeling sorry
for her.

She shuddered at the thought—no, far better to
struggle on, disguising her feelings, hopes and desires,
and trying desperately, on this trip at least, to forget
Nurra and his dead wife.

Jabir suddenly turned the wheel, and their vehicle left
the desert route and moved on to a scrub track.
'Exactly where are we?' Sara asked, as they bumped
over the uneven surface.

'This area is called the Wadi Kubbar. In the early
spring, when the rains come, it suddenly bursts into
life—becoming completely green. The desert isn't really
all sand, Sara,' Jabir turned his head to smile at her.
'The Israelis proved what miracles water can accomplish
in the desert.'

He drove on for a few minutes, then said, 'The place
we are going to is called the Zahra Palace. It belonged
to my mother, and my father gave it to me about seven
years ago. I hope you like it—it has been a place of
much peace and refuge for me.'

Sara turned sharply at the rough and abrasive tone in
his voice. The rays of the setting sun threw his bone
structure into dark relief, and he looked fiercely
hawklike as he stared blindly through the windscreen.

Why should he have needed peace and refuge during
the last seven years? She sighed as she realised that there
was so much about him she didn't know, and probably
never would.

'Is it like the King's Palace?' she asked, after a long
silence between them.

'No. As you'll see, it's really very small. My mother
came upon it by chance, when she was out hunting
with my father. It was a derelict shell, but she

restored it, and—well, you'll see—we should be there soon.'

She did indeed see, as the deep reddish-golden light of the dying sun lit up a glistening white building ahead of them, across the sands.

'Oh, Jabir,' she breathed softly, as they drew nearer to the building, 'it's—it's simply lovely! The walls seem to be glistening—they *are* glistening! It's as though they're covered with diamonds. It's fantastic!'

She grabbed his arm in excitement, as they came to a stop outside the Palace, which was like a Moorish castle with pointed arches and battlemented walls.

Jabir laughed at her. 'I'd like my arm back, Sara, if you've finished with it!'

She blushed as she realised she had completely forgotten where she was. 'But the walls...?' she said confusedly. 'They really do sparkle—I don't understand...?'

'My mother got the idea from the Wadi Hadhramat,' he said, getting out of the vehicle and coming around to open her door. 'It's a very fertile valley in what is now South Yemen, and rich merchants used to retire there to spend their last days—and their ill-gotten gains. Many of their houses had tiny pieces of glass mixed into the final outside coating of mortar. I'm sorry it's not diamonds, Sara!'

'What a beautiful idea. It's—it's like a welcoming beacon across the sand,' she said slowly, as she stood gazing with pleasure at the Zahra Palace.

Jabir looked at her startled for a moment, before saying, 'Come, we can't stand here all day, let us go in.'

Sara followed him through the large white wooden gates set in a Moorish arch, and entered into an enchanted world. The palace was built in a square, with a large garden shaded by trees, in the centre. The rooms all seemed to face into the garden, and were screened by lattice shutters, under a deep verandah which ran around the four sides of the square.

Jabir stood watching Sara intently as she gazed at the

scene in front of her. She stood as if in a trance, then very slowly drifted across the garden to a wide open doorway, and disappeared inside. She came back to earth to find Jabir shaking her arm, and looking at her with concern.

'Sara! Are you all right?'

Feeling lightheaded and dizzy, she said, 'Yes, I'm fine ... I ...' She shook her head, perplexed. 'I don't understand it. I've been here before ...' she gave a shaky laugh, 'only of course I haven't. Oh, heavens, I do feel peculiar!'

She looked around the large living room in which she found herself—goodness knows how. She certainly didn't remember walking in there. It was all very odd, she really must pull herself together.

'I'm fine now, Jabir. Really I am,' she smiled. 'It must have been the long day, and the heat.'

'Undoubtedly,' said Jabir in a blank voice. 'I suggest that you go and sit down in the garden. I will ask Hamid to bring you a cool drink.'

After she had gone, he stood looking thoughtfully at the wall in front of him, for a long time. Above the fireplace, laid with logs ready to light against cold desert nights, there was a mosaic frame around a painted inscription—in Arabic. Ordered by his mother in the last few months of her life, translated it read, 'May this house be a welcoming beacon across the sands.' *The exact words used by Sara—in English—as she entered the Zahra Palace.*

Jabir found Sara sitting on a bench in the garden, in the dusk. 'How are you feeling, Sara?' he asked.

'It's so lovely here, so peaceful.' She laughed softly. 'I *know* it sounds mad, and I won't go on about it, but I *know* I've been here before. I don't mind ... I mean ...' she paused, 'I feel so at home here. So happy and content.'

'There are many secrets of life to which we have no answer. Who knows, Sara, this may be one of them,' said Jabir slowly, as they sipped their cool drinks and watched the stars come out in the desert night sky.

'Come,' he said, 'I will show you to your room, and you can wash and change before dinner. The resident staff here does not include a cook, so we are going to be at the mercy of Hamid's culinary skills!'

Sara's room was much smaller and far simpler than the one at the King's Palace, but she loved it immediately. She had a shower in the small marble bathroom attached, and looked through her clothes for something suitable to wear.

Jabir had announced that morning that she had no need to take Yashi with her on the trip. 'You are able to cope without a maid, Sara, and it is better to travel in the desert with a minimum of people.' It had seemed quite a reasonable thing to say at the time, but this palace, although small, had a considerable number of rooms, and it now all seemed a little odd.

The only dress which hadn't creased during the journey was a simple affair in dark blue silk jersey. Unfortunately its sleeves, while short, were tight, as was the low bodice, and as Sara struggled to do up her zip she realised just how easily and quickly she had got used to the ministrations of a maid. The plain fact is, she told herself sharply, you're in grave danger of becoming spoiled!

Jabir was standing in the garden and turned at her approach. She almost gasped at the sight of his tall commanding figure, completely dressed in black robes, heavily trimmed in thick gold braid. He wore no headdress, and the thin black material whispered about him as he moved towards her, taking her hand and raising it to his lips.

'My darling Sara,' he said in a thick voice, as he gazed down at his wife, 'you look—as usual—quite lovely.' Sara blushed, as he continued to look at her in silence, his hooded eyes devouring her with hungry intensity. 'Come,' he said at last, still holding her hand firmly in his, 'let us see what Hamid has managed to produce for dinner.'

It was a short walk across the garden, and Sara

floated on air all the way. He had called her 'my darling', and although she knew she was living in a fool's paradise, she simply didn't care—not tonight, anyway.

Later, as they sat sipping their coffee in the garden, she said with a smile, 'You were very unfair to poor Hamid. It was a delicious meal—maybe he should leave you and become a chef?'

'Allah forbid!' Jabir laughed. 'He is far too useful to me. I can always buy a chef, but I could never replace Hamid. We grew up together, and he is one of the few people who will tell me to my face when he considers that I am behaving badly.'

'Rare indeed!' agreed Sara, trying not to grin.

'Sara!' he chuckled, 'such irony—and from one so young!' He moved slightly along the seat and slipped an arm around her slim waist. She felt her heart begin to pound with nervous excitement, as she quickly tried to pick a safe topic of conversation.

'I—I've been wanting to ask you,' she said hurriedly, 'why only you and the King ... why you are the only people to wear gold headbands, while everyone else wears black ropes.'

'The King wears his because he is the King—and I wear mine as his eldest son,' he replied, drawing her closer to his side.

'Does that mean ... that you will become King after your father?' Sara asked breathlessly. She felt she was beginning to lose the thread of her questions, as she felt the warmth of his body through his thin robes.

'Maybe,' he said shortly. 'Nothing has been decided yet. It is up to the King, my father, to say what he wishes to be done. He can declare me his heir, if he decides to, or he can leave the matter until his death. In that case the members of my family will decide who is best fitted to take his place.'

'My God!' she cried in sudden consternation. 'That means that ... that I might have to be a queen. Oh God!'

Jabir threw back his head and roared with laughter. 'Please, Sara, remember it's "Oh, Allah" in this country! Don't tell me that we have discovered *yet another* thing my darling wife hasn't thought of! You are an unending source of amusement and delight to me,' he told her, placing a hand beneath her chin and raising her face to his in the moonlight. 'I can't wait to discover what else you haven't thought about, I can think of at least two more major items. Life with you, my Sara, is certainly not dull!'

The naked desire in his eyes made her feel quite weak, and she saw with relief that Hamid had approached to have a word with Jabir. They conversed rapidly in Arabic, before Jabir turned to her and shrugged apologetically.

'It appears that an old Bedouin friend has arrived. I must greet him and arrange for him to have a bed for the night—it is the custom.'

'That's . . . er . . . fine, Jabir. I'm feeling very tired in any case. I think I'll have an early night, if that's all right.' Sara slipped away through the garden to her room, entering it through the open french windows which gave on to the verandah.

Starting to undress, she soon discovered that she had a major problem on her hands, and hesitated before reluctantly going back into the garden, where Jabir was still talking to Hamid.

'Jabir,' she called, 'could you . . . could you help me a minute, please?'

'What's the trouble, Sara?' he asked, striding over to her.

She sighed with exasperation. 'It's my zip. I can't reach it, I think my sleeves are too tight. If only Yashi were here!'

'What a pity,' he said blandly. 'It would seem that you will have to rely on the help of your poor husband Sara.' His lips twitched in amusement, as she blushed with frustration at her predicament.

He followed her back into the bedroom. 'Turn around,' he said, 'and I'll see what I can do.'

She turned her back and swept up her long blonde hair, holding it on top of her head, as his warm fingers undid the clasp at the neck of her dress. She shivered as she felt him slowly draw the zip down towards her hips. Murmuring her thanks, she gasped as she felt his hands slip inside the opening of her dress and clasp her waist, lightly pulling her against his hard frame.

He gave a long shaking breath, against her soft neck, as his hands moved up to cup her breasts with possessive fingers. Sara swayed helplessly against him, melting into his arms, as he whispered huskily in her ear, 'There is no need to thank me, my lovely Sara.'

'Jabir, I . . .' she murmured in a daze, desperately trying to clutch her dress, as he gently withdrew his hands from her body and swiftly left the room.

Left alone, she quickly slipped out of her dress and into a thin silk nightdress, still nervously excited from Jabir's caress. How long could she hope to hold him at bay, and hide her love, when her body longed so desperately for his touch?

She fell at last into an exhausted sleep, only to be woken some time later by a faint sound. She slowly opened her drowsy eyes, to see through the dim moonlight the broad bare shoulders and gleaming eyes of her husband, as he leant over her.

Her startled gasp was silenced as his mouth claimed hers. His soft, sensual kiss ignored her puny efforts to repulse him, as the weight of his warm body pinned her firmly down on the soft bed. Her struggles grew weaker as he quietened the body quivering beneath him with soothing strokes, at once tender and dominating.

At last she became quiescent, and it was then that he began to make love to her, slowly and gently, with a measured skill and experience that left her helpless against his deliberate arousal of the erotic tide of desire which flowed through her body. Her only instinct now was to respond to the delicate touch of his hands, and she moaned with submission as she moved sensually beneath him.

With slow, unhurried movements, Jabir removed her nightdress, his mouth tracing its passing with a lingering pleasure. 'So beautiful,' he muttered, his voice low and husky with passion, as he devoured her with his eyes in the dim light.

Her hands investigated the smooth skin of his broad shoulders, and moved to the warm male expanse of his chest, roughened slightly by the fine dark hair, before she put her arms around his neck, pulling him down towards her with hungry urgency.

'Sara!' he groaned, as his mouth possessed her lips, and she became a willing slave to his mounting passion. His hands continued to explore every secret part of her body, but more demanding, rousing. Great waves of passion shook and overwhelmed her, until at last he brought them both to an earth-shattering climax.

Sara awoke the next morning to find the bed beside her empty—Jabir had gone. She lay back on the pillows as she remembered the long passionate night. Twice more, before dawn, he had reached out for her, and each time she had wantonly responded. She blushed as she recalled the third time, when *she* had woken him . . .

A strange servant brought in her breakfast tray, and as Sara munched her roll and sipped the hot tea, she realised that her surrender to Jabir last night had placed her fairly and squarely on the horns of a dilemma.

What had happened had not changed the love she had for him, rather it had deepened and enriched it immeasurably. The dilemma lay at the core of her newly aroused sexuality. Already she found herself thinking ahead to the coming night. Even now, her body was becoming hot with desire at the thought of another night of passion.

How could she possibly hope to disguise her love, when every fibre of her being was going to be expressing it all too clearly? Sara gave a deep sigh. She knew that it would be impossible—and yet the thought of repulsing Jabir, even supposing that she was able to do so, was more than she could bear.

She got slowly and stiffly out of bed and went to have a shower. She had just finished dressing when Jabir knocked on the door and entered the bedroom. 'Good morning, Sara. I trust you slept well?'

Her startled eyes flew to his face, but she could read nothing in his bland expression. He—he knows very well just how I slept! she thought. Why is he pretending that nothing has happened? Puzzled, she looked at Jabir. He was wearing what looked, at first sight, like a Russian Cossack's outfit. Black loose trousers tucked into riding boots were topped by a black, high-necked tunic, his waist clasped by a wide leather belt. He looked so incredibly handsome that she felt quite weak and acutely conscious of the unmade bed behind her.

'I thought we'd take a picnic and go riding today,' he was saying, as she tried to bring her wayward thoughts under control. 'Can you ride, Sara?'

'Yes, but not very well. I'm no good at jumping and that sort of thing.'

'Truly?' he smiled at her. 'I was fooled by your ability to swim. I should hate to find myself engaged in a race under the hot desert sun!'

'I promise you,' she said, blushing slightly under his intense gaze, 'that I won't fall off too often. I really can't say more than that. I'm no great shakes at riding—truly.' She paused, struck by a sudden thought. 'Can I go dressed as I am?'

Jabir looked at his wife as she stood before him wearing a red and white checked cotton shirt tucked into her slim jeans. 'You could, but I think you will be more comfortable dressed as I am. I will send Hamid over with some clothes that I used to wear when I was a boy—they should fit you.' He turned to go.

'Jabir, I . . .' Surely he was going to say something—anything—about last night? Surely he couldn't expect them to act as strangers, not after they had spent such . . . such a night together?

'Yes, Sara,' he said, glancing at his watch. 'What is it? I don't want us to start off too late. We must reach the shade of the oasis for lunch, otherwise the heat will be too fierce.'

No, she told herself miserably. No, he wasn't going to say anything. His impersonal glance, his voice empty of any expression other than impatience with their delay, made that quite clear.

She felt suddenly angry, and her pride came to her rescue as she said, with a determinedly bright smile, 'It really doesn't matter, Jabir. It was nothing of any importance—nothing at all. If you'll just send over the clothes I'll change as fast as I can.'

Despite its inauspicious beginning, the day gathered momentum, and Sara found she was enjoying herself as they rode slowly across the desert. 'Very attractive indeed,' had been Jabir's comment on her appearance at the stables in his borrowed clothes, and as he helped her down from her horse at the shady oasis, the gleam was back in his lazy eyes. They ate their sandwiches, then Jabir showed her how to work the ancient well, drawing up the crystal-clear water from what seemed to be miles underground.

'It's so cold!' she gasped. 'I don't know why, but I expected it to be warm water down there.' Jabir laughed, and he occupied the rest of the journey, as they wound their way homewards, telling her about the ancient ways of the Bedouin tribesmen. Especially about their skill in tracking men and beasts. How they could tell from a camel's traces where it had come from, where it was heading, what sex it might be and even its colour.

'I don't believe it,' she laughed.

'I am, in fact, telling the truth,' Jabir assured her. 'My father sent me off, when I was twelve, to live for a year with our family tribe. I had a wonderful time, certainly one of the happiest of my life. I learned to wear rough clothes, to ride and hunt and survive on a handful of dates and a bowl of camel's milk. If all else fails me,' he laughed, 'I can catch our supper!'

Sara looked at her husband, relaxed and happy as he

reminisced about his boyhood. If only it could always be like this, she thought wistfully. Just the two of them, and the wide open spaces of the desert—the desert she was coming to love so much.

'The only claim I never saw proved,' he said, 'was the tribesmen's boast that they could tell from a woman's footsteps whether she was a virgin or not.' Sara glanced quickly at his completely expressionless face, and was about to ask how they were supposed to know that, when she saw his eyes dancing with amusement.

'You rotten liar!' she laughed, and brought her riding stick sharply down on his horse's rump. His beast leapt forward, and taken by surprise, Jabir was nearly unseated before he brought his mount under control again. Sara was laughing so much that she, in her turn, nearly fell off and had to be rescued by Jabir.

'It's lucky I'm such a gentleman, or I'd take a stick to your behind!' he smiled, helping her to sort out her reins. 'Come on, we must make sure we get back before dark. Only madmen and fools travel the desert at night.'

They reached the Zahra Palace just as the sun was setting, and after such an exhausting day Sara excused herself at the end of their evening meal, and retired to her room. She undressed and, not bothering with her nightgown, crawled gratefully and wearily into her bed. She was too tired, as she lay between the cool sheets, to even think about Jabir's odd behaviour in completely ignoring their lovemaking of the night before, and moments later she fell into a deep sleep.

She was awoken some time in the night, to find herself locked in Jabir's arms, as he slowly kissed the corners of her sleep-filled eyes. He ran his mouth gently down her cheek and took possession of her soft lips, as he teased her body with his fingertips in a featherlight touch that left her breathless with desire.

Slowly he withdrew his mouth, and lay looking down at her in the moonlight that streamed through the latticed window.

'Tell me that you want me,' he said in a soft voice, as his fingers continued to caress her body. 'Please, Sara, tell me that you want me.'

Sara couldn't speak for a moment, as she lay looking up at her husband. She was aware only of his dark, gleaming eyes, as full of desire as her own.

'Tell me!' he insisted softly.

'Oh . . . yes . . . yes!' Hungry for his touch, she moved her hips sensually beneath him as she returned his intimate caresses, with all the sexual vigour of her young body.

'My passionate little virgin!' he whispered thickly, as with a deep groan of desire his mouth plundered her breasts.

She gasped and moaned as his lovemaking, more roughly sensual and demanding than the previous night, took possession of her senses. She felt herself drowning in an avalanche of exquisite sensations such as she had never known before, and as he brought her to fulfilment, she cried out as great shudders ran through her slim frame.

CHAPTER EIGHT

SARA stood watching the guests as they crowded around Hassa, showering her with kisses and congratulations. It had been a lovely wedding, and the bride looked beautiful. It was a hot night, but the breeze from the sea made it very pleasant to be out in the private garden of the Palace. She looked around anxiously for Nadia, who as the youngest bridal attendant had behaved perfectly and was now chattering away to Hassa's mother, under the beady eye of Nanny Scott.

It was a week since they had returned from the magical trip to the desert, and already Sara felt stifled by the hothouse atmosphere of the Palace. The emotional currents criss-crossed, mostly above her head, but giving her a feeling of vague uneasiness and depression.

Jabir had left immediately they arrived back, on a business trip to Abu Dhabi, and she had concentrated on her Arabic lessons and the children. Her contact with Hassa had been limited as the date of the girl's wedding drew near. However, Nurra sought her out daily—generally when Sara was alone in the gardens, or one of the courtyards.

Always, without fail, she would at some part of the conversation mention her sister Miriam. I don't suppose she can help herself, Sara thought miserably. It's natural to miss one's sister, especially one so lovely and talented as Jabir's first wife. Day after day, Nurra spoke of her perfections: her beauty, her kindness and, above all, how she and Jabir had loved each other.

Sara wasn't a fool. Her reasoning and common sense told her that no one could be so perfect, and yet as the days passed, the insidiously soft low voice of Nurra

122

became almost the only one she heard. Each succeeding day Sara became more and more depressed at her own inadequacies, her own human failings, as compared with those of the incomparable Miriam. Without Jabir's presence, Sara began to lose her confidence, and to forget the magical ecstasy of their lovemaking in the desert.

No wonder she still lives for Jabir, she tormented herself night after night, as she lay alone in her bed. Miriam's becoming alive for me too!

As she twisted and turned during the hot and lonely nights, she was desperately aware of the terrible position in which she found herself. How could she compete against such a paragon? Jabir might have neglected his wife before she died, only to discover too late how much he loved her. But how much more he must love her now. Passing time would have given her a saintly loveliness in his eyes and, as the years progressed, it could only increase.

Those passionate nights in the desert now seemed as if they had never been. Maybe they hadn't, she thought feverishly. Maybe they were a fragment of her imagination? Jabir had, on each occasion, come to her bed when she was asleep and had left her before she woke. Never, at any point, had he alluded to their passionate lovemaking during the succeeding days.

However, in almost every other respect it had been a magical time for Sara. Her love for Jabir had grown deeper with each passing day, as different facets of his personality unfolded in the peaceful surroundings of the Zahra Palace.

Hesitantly at first, he had gradually begun to talk about his innermost feelings. Not very much, to be sure, but enough for her to feel that their relationship might be beginning to be built upon a more secure foundation than she had believed possible.

On the morning after their riding expedition, she had gone exploring through the lovely rooms, while Jabir had worked in his study. It must have been her shout of laughter that brought him to her, where he found her shaking with mirth as she looked around the room.

It was, technically, a room, although half of it was a swimming pool. She had found it on unlocking a small door in her bedroom, and she saw that another small door on the other side connected with Jabir's room. It was set in a corner of the square palace, and had no windows, only a domed glass roof.

The walls! What could one say? she had thought as she had caught Jabir's raised eyebrow.

'That door should not have been opened. This is not at all a suitable place for you,' he had said firmly.

'Jabir, don't be such a bore!' she had laughed in his face. 'Of course it's a suitable place for me—I'm supposed to be married, aren't I?' and she had laughed again as she surveyed the walls.

Obviously painted a long time before his mother had found the Palace, the painted walls were a tribute to love—joyous, happy and laughing love. Fat gentlemen in considerable undress were looking at, chasing after, or had caught some of the prettiest undressed fat ladies imaginable. Set in a painted landscape with gazelle, birds and hunting dogs, they filled the room with such an innocent gaiety that Sara laughed again.

'They're lovely! So sweet and charming. Why, it's one of the cleanest paintings I've ever seen. Really, Jabir! If you think these,' she gestured to the walls, 'if you think these are rude, then all I can say is you must really have a mind like a sewer!'

She turned to see Jabir grinning. 'They are charming, aren't they? They were the only part of the building still in good repair when my mother found it.' He laughed. 'I remember Scotty telling me that my father was very shocked when he first saw them, but my mother apparently reacted like you, and insisted on keeping them.'

She went over to the edge of the pool, and looking down saw the blue mosaic tiles beneath the water. It all looked so clean and cool that it gave her an idea.

'Do let's have a swim, Jabir.' She saw him hesitate, and added, 'You never know, it might give you some ideas—in the daytime for a change!'

He walked over to her and took her by the shoulders. Looking up into his face, she could have sworn that his eyes flashed with passionate desire, and wanting him to kiss her, she leant against his body in an open invitation.

The next thing she knew, she had been pushed backwards into the pool and was standing in four feet of water.

'What the ...?' She swept the long wet hair from her face in astonishment, to see Jabir standing by the edge of the pool, doubled up with laughter.

'I thought ...' he said, when he could catch a breath, 'I thought you needed cooling off!'

Sara, while overjoyed to see him so unusually relaxed and enjoying himself, decided that she really couldn't let him get away without some retaliation on her part.

'Well! I certainly won't proposition you again,' she smiled, wading towards him. 'Help me out, Jabir, please.'

He bent down to give her his hand, which she grasped firmly in both of hers, before giving him a sharp tug. 'Ah—h!' he cried, as he measured his length in the water, before surfacing beside her, to shake himself like a dog.

'You baggage!' he laughed. 'Look at me, I'm absolutely soaked!'

'Serve you right,' she said with a grin, turning away to climb out of the pool.

He caught her arm and pulled her roughly into his arms. 'Won't you, Sara?' he asked, with a sudden hungry intensity, as he buried a hand in her long wet hair, forcing her head back and tilting her face towards his. 'Won't you proposition me?'

'Jabir, I ...' she gasped huskily, as he stared fixedly down into her eyes.

'No, I don't suppose you will,' he said abruptly,

letting her go suddenly as if certain of her rejection.
'Come on, we must get out of these wet clothes.'

Sara's unhappy eyes followed him from the room,
and sighing deeply, she trailed miserably into her
bedroom to change. Later, still feeling upset, she went
to sit in the garden, hoping to calm her troubled mind.

The garden had worked its magic and she had spent
the rest of the day, while Jabir worked in his study,
exploring the Zahra Palace and meeting the servants
who lived there as the permanent staff.

In the early evening Jabir had suggested that they go
for a drive, and the Land Rover had swept across the
dunes, coming to rest by a small group of trees. He
jumped down and came around to open her door and
help her alight on to the desert sand, still warm from the
heat of the day.

He opened the back of the vehicle and removed some
bundles and a wicker basket. He swiftly unrolled the
bundles to display a woven silk carpet, on which he
threw some silk cushions.

Later, as they sat lounging against the soft cushions
and sipping clear amber tea from little glass cups set on
a silver tray, Jabir sighed with contentment.

'To understand us Arabs,' he said with a slow smile,
'you must first understand our deep feelings for the
desert. It is the source of everything we hold most
dear—our religion, our ancestry and our way of life. It
is where we have come from and where we shall lie,
finally. We do not exist happily if we are away from it
for too long.'

Sara sat quietly watching the deep undulations of the
sandy dunes, which seemed to stretch into infinity. 'It's
so still, so silent,' she said softly.

Tonight, out here in the desert, she was deeply and
sensitively aware of Jabir. The way the soft breeze
flicked his dark hair tipped with silver at the temples,
the tiny flecks of golden sand on his bare arms, the
slightest shifting of his powerfully lean body.

The desert air seemed to carry with it a soothing

balm for all troubled spirits, she thought as she sat watching the deep red ball of the sun slowly descend to the rim of the horizon. Feeling Jabir's eyes on her, she turned to smile gently at him. Time and motion seemed to stand still as they gazed into each other's eyes.

'Do you want to rule this desert land of yours?' she asked softly. 'Do you want to succeed your father as King?'

'*Insh'allah*—it must be as God wills, Sara.' He paused to look into the distance. 'However, the answer is yes, although perhaps rule is the wrong word. To care for my people is of more concern to me. You see,' he turned to her, 'anyone can rule, with varying degrees of success, but to care about eradicating poverty, to care enough to see that the wealth of this country is spread more evenly—that is what is really important. You understand?'

'Yes, I do, Jabir,' she said, looking at the quiet determination on her husband's face.

They sat in companionable silence, sipping their hot tea, as day gave way to night. Jabir lay back against the cushions, his hands folded beneath his head, as he stared at the stars in the sky.

'I wanted us to have some time on our own, Sara. A chance to get to know each other better. Which is why,' he turned to smile faintly at the girl lounging beside him, 'why we do not have the children or Yashi with us.'

'I had managed to work that out for myself, Jabir,' she grinned down at him. 'You are a great manipulator of people, you know.'

'Sara!' he chuckled in mock indignation. 'How can you say such a thing?'

'Very easily—O Master! There you go, striding through life—a command here, a click of your finger there. We slaves have a hard time of it . . .'

He smiled lazily up at her. 'Are you really my slave, Sara?'

'What else?' she answered as lightly as she could,

looking down at his face. His dark eyes gleamed enigmatically above the angular planes of his cheek-bones, thrown into prominence by a shaft of moonlight slanting through the leaves of the tree above.

He sat up, reaching forward to run his fingers through the heavy curtain of her long blonde hair. 'The moon's beam has turned your hair to silver—O Slave,' he said softly.

Sara shivered nervously as his hand moved to brush some particles of sand from her cheek. Her eyes widened in dismay when, as if in response to her reaction, he abruptly dropped his arm and turned away.

'Jabir, I . . .' She watched helplessly as he rose and walked slowly to the edge of the small oasis, to stand staring out at the desert. Aching with love, she gazed at his tall figure silhouetted against the night sky. With every fibre of her being she longed for his embrace, to feel his arms about her, to tell him how deeply she loved him . . . She sighed unhappily and stood up, brushing the sand from her clothes.

'It's a beautiful night, Sara,' said Jabir, turning to smile normally at her. 'The sky is so clear that it is not difficult to see Orion's Belt and the Great Bear amongst the stars.'

She walked towards him and they stood silently together, looking out over the sand-dunes at the starlit sky, the breeze rustling the leaves of the trees behind them. 'I wish we could stay here in the desert for ever,' she whispered.

'Alas, we cannot,' he said gently. 'And we must return now, or Hamid will send out a search party for us.'

His lovemaking that night was slow, tender and delicate, and of such an aching sweetness that she couldn't believe it was possible to feel such ecstasy. Once again, as on the previous night, he asked her to tell him that she wanted him, and once again she had responded with ardour.

Sitting in the garden the next morning she had heard

a noise in the sky, and a helicopter appeared, hovering overhead before landing outside the Palace. Hamid ran through the gates and returned carrying a black bag, as the helicopter lifted off into the sky again.

Presently Jabir came out into the garden carrying some papers, and an envelope. 'I've just had some mail delivered, and there's a letter for you, Sara. Unfortunately, while there was an outside chance that we could stay here a little longer, I now hear that we must leave tomorrow.'

'Oh, Jabir,' she said sadly.

'I know, but it can't be helped. I have to fly to Abu Dhabi tomorrow evening. I'm sorry, but there it is.'

She sat and read her letter, looking up smiling. 'It's from Ann. She says: "You will be amazed to hear that your father has decided to make an honest woman of me, and we're to get married next week. We've found a lovely cottage at Sandwich in Kent, right by the golf course—where else?"' Sara looked up from the letter. 'I'm so glad. She'll make my father very happy.'

'What day does she say they are getting married?' asked Jabir. 'We should send them a telegram of good wishes.'

'I don't know, let me see . . . no, there's no date, she just says, "Always remember that we'd love to see you whenever you can visit this country, and if you can't make it to Kent, I—never averse to the fleshpots of London—will come and stay with you in your hotel. I'm told the Princess Sara suite is out of this world! Love, Ann".'

Sara looked up, puzzled. 'What does she mean, my hotel? The Princess Sara suite?' She turned back to the letter. 'I'll read it again, it must be her writing . . .'

'No,' said Jabir, as he sorted through the papers on his lap, 'she's quite right. It is your hotel, and I'm glad to hear that your personal suite is ready for you.'

'What! You're joking?'

Jabir sighed and put down his papers. 'My dear Sara, what do I want with a hotel? Of course it's yours. We will stay there soon, I hope, and,' he added grimly, 'I profoundly hope that the bathwater will be hotter than it used to be!'

'What do you want with a hotel?' Sara repeated his words. 'But you bought it, for heaven's sake!'

'Only in order to marry you,' he replied serenely.

'Yes, and I wish you'd tell me why,' she said before she could stop herself.

'But, my dear wife, I gave you several good and valid reasons at the time, did I not?'

'Yes,' she said heavily. 'Yes, you did.'

Jabir put down his papers to regard her through heavy-lidded eyes. 'What other reasons could I possibly have had?'

'None, of course,' said Sara, in a small voice, looking down blindly at the letter in her hands. 'I—I suppose I should say thank you—about the hotel, I mean. But sometimes I wish—I wish you'd never come near the place!' she cried, and jumping up, she had run weeping to her bedroom.

She was lying crying on her bed, when Jabir walked in and came over to sit beside her. 'My Sara,' he said, gathering her up into his arms, 'are you very unhappy with me?'

Despite the pain of living with a man who didn't love her she couldn't bear the thought of her life without him. 'No, Jabir, I'm not unhappy with you,' she whispered. 'But . . .'

'. . . but sometimes your new life is confusing—yes?'

She nodded, as he wiped her eyes. 'I'm also,' she sniffed, 'I'm also not very happy about going back to the King's Palace. I'm sorry, Jabir, I know it's your home, but I wish—oh, how I wish we could live here, in the desert.'

'Alas, we cannot. Come, cheer up. You are perhaps homesick? Maybe we will have your father and Ann to stay, yes?'

I'm not homesick, she thought heavily, I'm just sick with love for you. A tear trickled down her cheek as she answered. 'Yes, I'd love to see them. I'm sorry to be so silly.'

As the day had passed, she had grown more and more edgy at the thought of leaving the desert palace and their return to the capital, and Nurra. She began, also, to feel increasingly depressed and resentful of the way Jabir was treating her. How could he make such passionate love at night, and pretend that nothing had happened during the day?

She had worked herself up into such a state of nerves that when he came to her that night she was awakened by his step on the floor and scrambled out of bed, trying to escape.

He caught her by the window, and sweeping her up in his arms threw her on to the bed. She fought him, wildly and fiercely, for all she was worth. But her kicks and struggles were futile against his superior strength, as he calmly pinned her to the bed, while he tore off her nightgown as if it were a piece of paper.

'I don't want you—why can't you leave me alone!' she sobbed, as she felt herself growing weak and exhausted by the fight.

Jabir's mouth moved possessively over her throat and along her shoulders, as his hands cupped her already roused breasts. 'Oh yes, you do, Sara!' he whispered as he began to gently coax her to such a pitch that she forgot why she had tried to fight him. Once again his mouth and strong body worked their power, and she abandoned herself to the passionate desire which he was always able to evoke in her.

Falling asleep in his arms later, she had murmured, 'Please don't leave me.'

'I'll never leave you, Sara—never.' His arms had tightened around her, but she was fast asleep and didn't hear his words.

He was gone the next morning, as always, and she had surprised herself and him by crying in the Land Rover as they left. 'I feel so unhappy at leaving this place,' she had sobbed, as he passed her a handkerchief, softly reminding her that Hamid was sitting behind them. 'I can't help it, Jabir, really I can't. It's like a terrible pain in my heart ... I don't know why. I'm looking forward to Hassa's wedding, but ...' she cried quietly, gradually calming down as they travelled further away from the Zahra Palace.

Watching Hassa now, looking so radiant, Sara ached with envy. Why did Jabir only come to her in the dark, and leave before daylight? Why? Why? She could see no rhyme or reason for him to deny so firmly in the day what he had demanded so strongly at night. He had been more than frank about the normal sexual attraction between a man and a woman, why then did he pretend that nothing had happened between them?

If only—if only I could be as happy as Hassa, she thought miserably, instead of being trapped in some sort of devilish nightmare, from which there seemed no escape.

She saw Nanny Scott across the room and decided to go and talk to her. Maybe plain Scottish common sense would help to take her mind off her problems.

'Hello, Scotty,' she said, 'isn't Nadia looking pretty, and she's been behaving so well.'

'Aye, so far!' Miss Scott said darkly. 'I daren't take my eyes off her for a moment, or the good Lord knows what she'll get up to.' She patted the seat beside her. 'Rest your feet, my dear. These weddings go on for ever, I must have been to hundreds, and they're all the same.'

'I knew I've been meaning to ask you something. You came out to Assir with Jabir's mother, didn't you?'

'Poor Miss Zahra,' the old nanny sighed. 'Och! What a to-do there was when she told her father she was going to marry an Arab prince! You wouldn't credit the fuss. Cut her off without a shilling, he did. I was her maid, you know, and she asked me to come here with her. She was frightened of being homesick, you see. Well, I had no family—nothing to keep me in England—so off we went.'

'What was she like, Scotty?'

'Like you,' was the simple reply. 'How Master Jabir, who never saw his poor mother—there aren't even any photographs of her, the King was that upset he tore them all up when she died—how he picked her spitting image, I'll never know. Even your name is like hers. When you came into the schoolroom that first day—well, you could have knocked me over with a feather!'

Sara smiled. 'I meant what was she like—her character?'

'She wasn't a plaster saint, you know. But she had such a loving nature, that's what I will always remember. My word, the laughs we had in this godforsaken and heathen land! We'd never seen such insects—and the flies . . .! Things have improved since those days, I'll say that. Prince Abdul—well, the King as he is now—my word, he was nuts about her. And she—well, she just worshipped him. Lovely, it was.' Scotty took out a handkerchief and blew her nose loudly. 'Ah well,' she sighed. 'It's so nice to see history repeating itself!'

'Oh, Scotty, I don't think . . .'

'Don't be silly, dear,' Scotty said briskly. 'My Master Jabir, he's mad about you—and don't tell me you don't care about him. I wasn't born yesterday. And look,' she added, pointing across at Jabir, who was talking to a group of Arab guests from neighbouring countries. 'Don't try and tell me he isn't going to be King in his turn. I've been around this court for a long time, and I know what's what!'

'Oh, Scotty, do you really think so?' Sara asked anxiously. The thought of having to be Jabir's Queen filled her with dread.

'Certain sure,' came the emphatic answer. 'Well, it's as plain as the nose on your face—who else is there? I know the King wanted to tie it all up with that brazen hussy Nurra. Nasty bit of work, dear, best leave her alone, if you'll take my advice. Still, the Palace is buzzing that the King's fair gone on you, and as pleased

as Punch at the way things have turned out; so that's all
right and tight.'

Sara was sunk in her own miserable thoughts when a
lazy voice came from behind them. 'How's my favourite
nanny?'

'Master Jabir! How you made me jump. We've been
having a nice cosy chat.'

'Well, I'm about to interrupt it, I'm afraid.' He turned
to Sara, 'I've had a call from John Morgan, who is in
Paris. Some business deals have suddenly come to
fruition, and we must leave for Europe tomorrow. It is
likely that we shall be away for some weeks, and so I must
leave now. There are people I have to see before we go.'

'Europe? Tomorrow?' Sara was taken aback.

'Yes, and possibly America as well. You will, of
course, wish to say goodbye to my sister. However,
since you have your cases to pack, I would advise you
not to stay too long. Hamid is waiting outside to escort
you back to the house.'

'Really, Jabir! I can walk across the garden by
myself, surely?'

She was surprised by his curt instructions. He had
only returned back from his business trip in time to
change quickly, before the wedding. They had hardly
exchanged more than a word or two then, and none
since the start of the reception. What was wrong now?

'Hamid will be waiting,' he said shortly, before
turning to leave.

Sara followed his departure with troubled eyes.
Something had upset him, but what? Sighing, she said
goodbye to Miss Scott and started moving through the
crowd towards Hassa.

Nurra, looking as beautiful as ever, glided over to her
side. She never seems to walk like the rest of us,
thought Sara, she just appears to flow.

Nurra's low voice cut into her thoughts. 'I've just
been having a lovely long talk with Jabir. He tells me he
only returned this morning—just in time for the
wedding.'

'Yes,' said Sara. 'He works too hard.'

'And you're off tomorrow, I hear, for a long trip. What a busy life you're going to be leading! Still, that's a good thing, isn't it?'

'A good thing?' Sara asked absently, half her mind still worrying about what had upset Jabir. Nurra had apparently just been talking to him . . .

'Well—no, I shouldn't say anything. It's not fair on you.' Nurra's voice was full of sympathy. 'But Jabir does seem to be acting very oddly . . .' Her catlike eyes glinted at Sara. 'I mean—well, I feel sorry for you, that's all.'

'Jabir's acting oddly? How do you mean?' Sara looked at her anxiously.

Nurra shrugged. 'I know he misses Miriam, but for him to say that he thinks about her day and night—*especially the nights*—well, it doesn't sound very "sane", does it? I wouldn't have mentioned it to you, Sara, but he's said it to one or two other people, and you know what this place is like! That's why I thought it would be good for you both to be away for a bit.'

Sara stared at Nurra, the blood draining from her face.

'I do want to be helpful, Sara,' purred Nurra, 'and I gave him a good talking to. I told him that it wasn't fair on you. What sort of life is it for Sara, I said. If you go on like this, she will leave you—and who would blame her. I told him to talk to you about his problem, but he said he couldn't. He also said that he'd deny he'd ever said anything to me—of course.'

'Of course . . .' echoed Sara. The rich gold dress which Jabir had admired earlier in the day now weighed heavily on her shoulders, and her head began to ache. She suddenly couldn't take any more of Nurra, and her soft hypnotic voice, constantly reminding her of her hopeless love for Jabir. She wanted to run away and hide, but she knew she couldn't—not yet. With an almighty effort she bade Nurra goodnight and went over to see Hassa and the Queen.

Hamid was waiting, as instructed, to escort her home, and it was only when he left and Sara stood alone in the large empty hall that she could face the one emotion which filled her heart and mind to the exclusion of all else.

She was trembling with anger as she strode into the main living room, and across to the drinks cupboard. Furiously she poured a large neat whisky, and shaking with rage she marched up the marble stairs to her suite.

'Out!' she shouted at a startled Yashi, who fled the room.

'I'll kill him!' Sara cried aloud, as she tore off her gold dress and threw it over a chair. 'I'll kill him . . . kill him!' she chanted with uncontrollable fury, as she removed her underclothes and stalked into her bathroom.

Missed his wife, did he? Day and *night*, did he? she fumed as she switched on the shower. That . . . that apology for a man! Boiling in oil was too good for him!

She had begun to calm down, very slightly, as she struggled into a thin silk nightgown and sat at her dressing table, brushing her long hair with angry strokes.

It was one thing to be bought, she said to herself, and God knows she had fought against that, but it was quite another to be used the way Jabir had used her. Nurra had, tonight, merely confirmed what she had been unable to bring herself to accept this last unhappy week. Her husband had been thinking only of his dead wife when he had been making love to her!

She had called him a swine before, and she was right—only that was too good a word for the way she felt about Jabir!

She took a gulp of the whisky, and gasped as the fiery liquid burned her throat. No wonder he had never mentioned their lovemaking during the days they had been together—he hadn't been making love to her at all. Their passionate nights . . .? She writhed with agony and shame as she remembered her desire and eager, passionate response. How he must have laughed, as he had so professionally aroused her. What secret amusement he must have felt!

She resolutely tramped on the thought that his ardour had been genuine. Yes, there had been desire in his eyes, but 'all cats are grey in the dark' . . . and it was only in the dark that he had come to her.

It was a dreadful and wicked thing he had done. To use and abuse her in the way he had. Why couldn't he have picked some nice, mature woman with whom to indulge himself? He'd taken her virginity and it meant nothing to him. God, how she hated him! He was totally . . . totally amoral!

A door banged downstairs, and she heard him come upstairs and go to his rooms.

Right, Master Jabir, she thought with relish, as she sipped her drink, I'm going to tell you just where you get off, good and proper, as Scotty would say. I'm going to put the boot in, and keep kicking. Love and hate are supposed to be twin emotions, so they say. Well, let's just concentrate on the hate for a bit. She emptied her glass, and taking a deep breath, went to confront her husband.

Opening the door without knocking, she found Jabir sitting at his desk, looking through a pile of papers. He looked up startled at her entrance, then smiled.

'Good evening, Jabir,' she said, closing the door. The thin red silk of his dressing gown clung to his wide shoulders, and was partially open, displaying his broad chest. Sara felt a sudden weakening at the knees, and leant against the door for support. Just remember how you hate him, she told herself firmly.

'Come in, Sara,' he said. 'Did you enjoy the party? I'm sorry I had to leave early. Have you finished packing?'

'No, I didn't enjoy the party, and I didn't come here to talk about packed cases, either,' she said in a high clear voice she hardly recognised as her own.

'Really?' Jabir put down his papers and turned to survey his wife. His eyes ran over her figure, partially displayed to his view by the long black silk nightgown which clung to her slim form. He said, with a smile, 'Perhaps there was something else you wanted?'

'You're so damn right—there is!' She flushed at his glance and hitched up one of the thin straps of her gown, which had slipped down her arm. 'And it's not what you have in your dirty little mind, so you can take that smarmy look off your face right now!'

'I—what did you say?' he frowned.

'You heard! Tell me, Jabir,' she continued, 'would you say that you were an honourable man—in business, I mean? Having made an agreement, would you stick to it?'

'Of course. But I don't see . . .'

'You will, so just shut up and listen!' Her teeth began to chatter with tension as she saw his face flush at her words.

'We have a contract between us, don't we? Made at the hotel in London. Among your other business deals you may have difficulty in remembering it, but that was one where you bought a hotel, and also blackmailed Miss Sara Morrison into accepting your terms. To wit: look beautiful, act the good hostess, and be a mother to your children. Right?'

'Sara! What's the matter with you . . .'

'There's nothing wrong with me, it's the company I have to keep! Am I right?

'You must be drunk,' said Jabir, standing up.

'I wish I was—and I fully intend to be—but at the moment I've only had one whisky, and am in full control of my senses. Something I intend to remedy as soon as I've finished with you.'

'I didn't blackmail you, Sara.'

'Hah! O.K.—what's in a word? You can have coercion, emotional duress, immoral force, Hobson's choice—you name it, I don't care. The fact is I accepted your terms, and in return I, Sara Morrison, was granted unlimited luxury, my father was provided for, and I have tried, although I don't know how much I have succeeded, to bring some happiness into your children's lives. Right?'

'You've made my children very happy, I'm most grateful for that—you know it, Sara.'

'Stop flannelling me, and let's keep to the agenda—it beats me how you run any business, Jabir. I'm still asking whether the contract as outlined by me is correct—and sit down, I don't trust you one inch!'

'You look magnificent when you're angry, Sara.' His eyes gleamed at her, and he grinned as he sat down and folded his arms. 'You are technically correct in your assessment of the meaningful, viable and relevant scenario, as originally outlined between us. Is that businesslike enough for you, Sara?'

'If that rubbish means what I think it does, then we have a contract—and one about which we're agreed. Now, you say you're an honourable man? Really, you know, I feel like Mark Antony over Caesar's body . . . "but Brutus is an honourable man". Well, darling Jabir, jolly old Brutus killed Caesar. He got his knife in and twisted it—just like you!'

'Sara, I have absolutely no idea what you're talking about. Why don't you sit down and . . .'

'I'll stay where I am. You say you are an honourable man—what a laugh! So am I—an honourable woman, I mean. I will keep to our lousy contract just as long as I can, but,' she spoke slowly through clenched teeth, 'but *only* what I agreed to in London, and have outlined to you here tonight. Do you understand, or do I have to spell it out in four-letter words?'

Jabir sat very still for a moment. The hooded lids hid any expression in his eyes, as he said in a quiet voice, 'You wish, I take it, to have no further intimate contact with me?'

'Got it in one!—and so delicately put. Well done, Jabir. Always quick on the uptake, aren't you?'

'Sara, I . . .' He paused, then said slowly, 'May I ask why?'

'Ho! What a good question!' Sara was shivering

violently now, unable to control either her tongue or her anguish. 'My God! You really are a ... a swine!' She spat the words at him. 'I called you that once before, and how right I was. Making love to me, and all the time you were thinking of your dead wife! How can you ...'

'What!' Jabir jumped up from his seat and a moment later was standing over her, his hands clasped on her shoulders in a vicelike grip. 'What did you say?' he demanded, his face as white as chalk.

Sara was past caring what she said, as in her agony and torment she strove to hit back at the man whom she loved, and who had so cruelly duped her.

'I know all about you—you beast! I know you're still in love with your wife. How you must have laughed while you were busily seducing me in the dark, so you could pretend it was Miriam. It's horrible—it's ...'

'How dare you say such things!' Jabir was now as furious as Sara, and far more terrifyingly angry, as he stood back looking at her with blazing eyes.

'How dare I say it? Why not—apparently everyone else is! Ask Nurra, she's told me all about you and Miriam. How you think of nothing else but her—day and night—*especially the nights, apparently*! Go on, hit me,' she cried, as he raised his hand. 'You've done everything else to me—what's one more blow from such a loving, loving husband!' and totally overwrought, she burst into tears.

'Nurra? My God, that woman! Believe me, Sara,' he put his hands on her arms. 'You must believe me! Whatever she has said, it is not true.'

'It is all true,' she sobbed, the tears streaming down her face. 'I'm sorry about your dead wife—I'm sure she was as lovely as Nurra says she was. But you had no right to have used me the way you have. I believed what you said about ... about sexual attraction being normal. What a fool I was! You were thinking about Miriam all the time! That's why you only m-m-made love to m-me in the dark,' she sobbed. 'It's all true!'

'No, it isn't, you stupid woman!' He shook her roughly. 'It was because I . . . It was the only way to . . . Damn it, Sara!' his voice softened. 'You must know . . . you must realise by now that I . . .' and he clasped her in his arms and kissed her roughly with mounting passion.

Appalled, Sara realised that her treacherous body was responding to his firm embrace and inflaming kisses, as he pinned her against the door. He relaxed the pressure for a moment, and she ducked down and out from beneath his arms. As he turned to her, she slapped his face as hard as she could.

'I know nothing about you, and I now care even less,' she said, panting, as he stood in front of her, a hand to his face. 'We both know what a good lover you are—you don't have to put on yet another demonstration for my benefit. Save it for someone who will appreciate your technique. We also both know,' she added bitterly, 'just what a push-over I was—like taking candy from a baby, wasn't it, Jabir?'

'Oh, my love . . .'

'Save it! I never was your love and I never will be. Ugh! The thought of your lovemaking makes my flesh creep. There's only one thing you have to remember— and don't ever make the mistake of forgetting it. Never, never touch me again, do you hear? *Don't ever touch me again!* If you do, I'll scream the place down and leave you—permanently!

Jabir stood looking at her for a long time, his face a blank mask. 'You have made yourself very clear, Sara. It shall be as you wish.'

He turned and walked slowly over to his desk, to stand with his back to her, looking blindly at the wall opposite. 'Leave me!' he commanded, in a harsh voice.

'Don't worry, I'm going. Just don't make the mistake of forgetting what I've said!'

Sara managed to stalk out of his room with her head high, and just made it to her own suite before she collapsed on her bed, to weep the night away.

CHAPTER NINE

THE justly famous view spread itself before Sara in all its panoramic glory, as she stood looking out of the window of the penthouse suite. She remembered an amusing film she had seen long ago, about a coachload of tourists who had visited nineteen countries in five days. She knew exactly how they felt, she thought, as she looked now at the skyscrapers of Manhattan—only it wasn't so funny in real life—in fact it was awful.

There was a knock at the door and John Morgan came in, accompanied by his female assistant who had been acting as Sara's secretary for the past three weeks.

'You O.K., Princess? You look kinda tired.' John looked with concern at the Prince's wife. She definitely wasn't the woman he'd first met in London. That woman had been still a girl, soft and feminine. He looked now at the perfectly groomed Princess, in her cream Chanel suit and blouse, who stood so still, so frozen, as she regarded him with a bleak look. She'd lost weight during the last three weeks, he thought, looking at her figure, and her eyes—the largest, bluest and most unhappy eyes he had ever seen.

'I'm fine,' Sara said shortly. 'What's the programme for today?'

'Pretty full, I'm afraid—so we'd better get this show on the road,' he laughed.

He gathered his papers together, in the stony silence which had met his small joke, and started to rattle off the schedule, her secretary making notes where necessary.

'O.K., here we go: first off, you and the Prince have a meeting at eleven a.m. with the Mayor. Remember it's New York, and the Jewish vote is important. But then so is their need for Arab investment money. However, the Prince is known to be one of the few Arab leaders who's not anti-Israel, and your English charm is expected to swing the meeting our way.'

'I'm always happy to be of some use,' she said, in a dry voice.

'Er ... yeah, right. Next, Princess, you lunch alone with the Daughters of the American Revolution. Celia here has your speech. You know the thing: lovely to be here ... great country ... can't wait to return, etc., etc.'

'Don't you think, John, that it might be nice—just for once—if we could try for a tiny drop of sincerity in these dreadful speeches you give me?' she asked him blandly.

'What? Oh sure, we'll stress the "sincere" bit. See to that, Celia. Now: two p.m. to three-thirty, trip up the Hudson River, by kind courtesy of Media Inc.—Right?'

'Wrong!'

'Wrong?' he said in bewilderment.

'Definitely wrong. Check my file. You will note that I'm apt to be sick on boats. I don't think Murder Inc. would be ...'

'Media Inc., for heaven's sake, Princess!' John laughed nervously, and wiped his forehead with a large handkerchief. 'O.K., O.K., I get your point. Scrub that, Celia, and telephone regrets. Where was I? Oh yes, three-thirty to four p.m., visit to the United Nations Headquarters, overlooking the East River. The Prince may be stuck in a business meeting, so be prepared to be on your own. However, the Assir Ambassador will be there to greet you. No speech, just a quick look round. Right?'

Sara remained silent.

'That just about wraps it up. The Prince is dining with the Press boys tonight, so you're free this evening.'

'Free? How kind—thank you. I see that the New York Philharmonic Orchestra are giving a concert at Carnegie Hall tonight. I'd like a ticket, please.'

'Well, I don't know ... The Prince might not ...'

'The Prince will neither know, nor will he care. I

intend to listen to some music tonight. See to it, please,'
Sara commanded.

'Yes, yes, of course, Princess.' John looked nervously
at the woman standing by the window. 'Is there . . .' he
cleared his throat, 'is there anything else I can do for
you?'

'Yes.' Sara turned her back to the two of them, to
look out of the window. 'I've been trying for the past
three days, while we've been here in New York, to make
an appointment to see my husband—alone. I would like
to have at least one hour of his undivided attention.
Have you made any progress? This is, after all, the third
day running I've had to make such a request.'

John glanced nervously at Celia, and shrugged.
'Yeah—sure. I think I've got a note on my desk.'

Still with her back to them, Sara said in a hard voice,
'Don't lie to me, please. Just—just arrange it. It's
important, for the Prince's sake, not my own.'

'I promise I'll do what I can, really I will.'

'I'm sure you will.' She turned round. 'I would also
like a chauffeured car ready here, outside the hotel, at
nine-thirty tomorrow morning.'

'But we're going to Harlem,' John protested. 'There's
this ethnic group of . . .'

'You may be going to Harlem, I'm going to the
airport. I'll say goodbye now, John and Celia. Thank
you for all your help, and I'm sorry it has to end this
way.' She turned back to look out of the window.
'Close the door when you leave, please.'

John hurried his assistant out of the room. 'Hell's
bells!' he leant against the closed door and wiped his
forehead. 'She's cracking up—and leaving. The Prince
is like a bear with a sore head. I can't talk to him any
more—something's got to be done, and fast! I'll go to
the other suite and have a word with Hamid, he's the
only one who has any influence with the Prince. You
hold the fort until I get back.'

Sara remained standing by the big window, as the
door closed, silent tears trickling unheeded down her

cheeks. 'Oh God! Help me, I . . .' she moaned as she leant her head against the cool glass. 'Somebody must be able to help me . . .!'

The trip had been an unmitigated disaster from the word 'go'.

They had been given the use of the King's Boeing 727 for their journey and they had boarded the aircraft, as they had driven from the Palace, in complete silence. Sara, who knew she looked like death after her sleepless night, went to the rear of the plane and chose one of the two bedrooms in which to rest. She took a sleeping pill provided by the stewardess, and mercifully fell asleep at last, only to be woken as they approached Paris.

How she got through the dinner party at Maxim's that night, she never knew. She could have wept all over the beautifully prepared food, instead of which she and Jabir had to pretend to be the loving couple they weren't.

Driving back to their hotel later, Jabir had pressed the button to close off the window between their chauffeur and themselves.

'If you are to keep to our contract, Sara, I'm afraid you will have to perform better than you did tonight.' His harsh voice came from the darkness, as he sat as far away from her as possible.

'Yes, Jabir,' she said in a small voice. 'I will try.'

'See that you do.' There was silence for a moment, then he said, 'Just to put your mind at rest, I have arranged for us to reside in separate suites on different floors, in the hotels where we stay. Marie has flown up from Cannes, and will be waiting for you at the hotel tonight. John Morgan has an assistant, Celia, who will act as your secretary. She will answer the telephone, write letters—anything you want.'

'Thank you, Jabir. I . . .'

The car drew up at the hotel as she spoke, and while the chauffeur held the door open, Jabir turned to her. 'I can see no need for any further communication between us. You will be given a briefing each day by John—that should suffice. If you have anything particular you wish to say to me, you may make an appointment through him. Goodnight, Sara,' and he stepped out of the car and went into the hotel.

That was how the trip had started, and it pursued its nightmare course through the succeeding three weeks. Paris—Bonn—Rome—Madrid—Tokyo—America. 'If it's Spain, it must be Friday!' said Sara, somewhat hysterically, to Marie one morning as the French girl dressed her hair for the day. What would she have done without her? Marie, not much older than herself, had been kindness itself.

Sara had shed many tears the first two weeks, and her maid was always at hand with a handkerchief and aspirin for the tension headaches which had begun to plague her. She never said anything to Marie about why she was in such distress, but then she didn't suppose the close members of their entourage had any doubts about the position between herself and Jabir.

Jabir—there was only one word for his behaviour— hellish! Nothing was ever right, in fact everything was always wrong. He snapped and shouted at everyone— everyone, that was, except Sara. For her he reserved an icy silence that was far more unnerving.

As she stood at the window, unable to stop the tears from falling, she knew she had come to the end. Yesterday she had sent a cable to her father, and despatched Marie to buy two tickets to London, since her maid had insisted on coming with her. Ann and her father might not be particularly pleased to see them, but that was just too bad. She had to get away, and there was nowhere else for her to go.

She had to see Jabir. They had to talk. As much as she hated-loved him, she had to tell him herself that she was going. If only to stop him sending out the police to find her, she thought wryly.

Sara was at breaking point, and knew it. The last week, especially, she had felt so deathly tired that it had become the most enormous effort to even get up in the mornings, after yet another sleepless night. She was terrified of taking sleeping pills; in her present state of mind she couldn't guarantee that she wouldn't do something stupid.

She rang for Marie. 'Some black coffee, please. I've got to get through another day somehow, so make it very strong.' As she drank the hot liquid, Sara reflected on the old joke that it was better to be rich than poor, because you could always be miserable in comfort. It certainly isn't true, she thought, and I ought to know, since I've tried it! At least, before, when I wasn't happy, I had plenty of things to occupy my mind. Anything, but anything, was better than spending one's days dressed up to the nines, totally isolated from the real world. I'm a vacuum-packed plastic doll, thought Sara in the depths of despair as she prepared to resume her day's schedule.

As always, she managed to stagger through the various events as outlined for her by John. The Mayor had been sweet, and the American ladies had been charming and the United Nations Building was interesting.

John had produced her concert tickets and the chauffeur drove her to Carnegie Hall, arranging to collect her later.

The last musical offering of the evening was the Elgar Cello Concerto. The mournful sounds of the cello exactly echoed her desolate heart, so much so that she had difficulty in controlling her emotions. At the conclusion she left hurriedly, running blindly to the waiting car. There was no difficulty in recognising it, it bore a small version of Assir's national flag. She opened the door, collapsing in tears as she threw herself into the back seat—and into Jabir's arms.

He held her tightly all the way back, gently stroking her hair, as she cried her heart out. She was still racked by sobs when the doctor arrived to examine her. There was a whispered consultation outside her bedroom door, and Jabir came in to sit on the bed beside her.

He took her in his arms, and as he gently rocked her to and fro she managed to stop crying and lie quietly against his chest.

'Sara,' he said softly, 'you must rest. We—we will go away tomorrow, and you will rest and get well.'

'I'm ... I'm going to London, tomorrow ...' The tears started again.

'No, not tomorrow. Later, if you wish. Now you need to rest.'

'Jabir,' she said, exhausted, 'what are you doing here? What about your dinner tonight? And all the arrangements?'

'I left early. Hamid and John said you were not well. Darling Sara, you've nearly had a nervous breakdown, so I've cancelled the rest of the trip. It's all right—I will make sure you rest and get well. Trust me. Yes?'

'Oh yes, Jabir,' she murmured, and fell asleep in his arms.

The morning sun slanted in through the latticed shutters and fell on Sara's face, as she slowly opened her eyes. Stretching drowsily in the large bed, she looked around her at the simple white walls and furniture. During the last few days, when she had been under such heavy sedation, she had known that she was in a place of peace and happiness. Now she sat up and realised fully for the first time that she was in her bedroom at the Zahra Palace. She also realised that she was ravenously hungry.

Before she could get out of bed, Marie knocked and entered the room. 'Oh, *madame*, you must not—you 'ave been so ill!'

'Nonsense, Marie, I feel terrific, and dying for some food—in fact I'm starving!'

Over the maid's protests, she insisted on getting out of bed, and although her legs felt a bit shaky, she was able to walk unaided to an easy chair by the open window.

'It's wonderful to be back here,' she said, taking deep breaths of the fresh desert air. 'What I'd really love is a hot bath, and then lots of toast and coffee.' As Marie hesitated, she smiled, 'I really do feel very well.'

Lying in the hot scented water, Sara felt really relaxed for what seemed the first time in the past month. She could remember the desperately unhappy three weeks of the business trip, but it all seemed so long ago. She had absolutely no recollection of the journey here, and only a hazy memory of the day—days in which, she realised, she must have been under sedation.

As the steam rose, so did her spirits. She was, once again, in the place where she felt happy, peaceful and relaxed. How had Jabir known . . .? Her mind sheered away from any thoughts about her husband. It was enough to be here and feeling well again.

Her stomach rumbled, reminding her of her need for food, and she climbed carefully out of the bath. Her legs still weren't very steady as, having dried herself and put on a thin white silk dressing gown, she walked slowly back into her room.

Despite her protestations, she succumbed to Marie's insistence that she get back into the freshly made bed. Sara realised that she did indeed feel tired, and not nearly as strong as she had thought. The maid placed the breakfast tray on her knees, and was genuinely pleased when she returned to find the plates empty.

'Marie, that was fantastic! I feel so full.' A thought struck her. 'What are you doing here in Assir? Surely you should be on the yacht in Cannes?'

'*Mais non, madame*. I say to ze Prince zat I come— *absolument!* He say O.K. Zis place is *très agréable*— verry nice—yes?'

'Oh yes,' Sara sighed happily. 'It certainly is absolutely *très bon*.' She laughed, 'My French is even worse than your English!'

Suddenly feeling tired, she told Marie she would rest for a bit before getting dressed. Lying back on the pillows, she turned her head to the window. The lattice shutters prevented her from seeing into the garden, but she knew it was there, and she felt content . . .

Opening her eyes, she realised that she must have slept for some time, because the sun no longer shone into the room. She lay, gazing idly, then saw that the chair beside the window now contained her husband.

Sara lay very still, watching him as he sat with his head bowed, reading a book. Jabir, his long legs stretched out in front of him, was wearing a pair of tight riding breeches and black shiny riding boots. Her eyes rose to take in his broad shoulders and wide chest clothed in a white, short-sleeved shirt, whose buttons were half undone displaying his warm creamy skin.

Her heart started to flutter nervously as she looked at his face bent over his book. Jabir's firm mouth and high cheekbones, set beneath his black hair tipped with silver at the temples, were all she could see from where she lay.

She closed her eyes as the fluttering in her heart spread to the rest of her body. What had happened between them strangely didn't seem to matter. She loved him—that was the beginning, the middle and the end of it all. She opened her eyes again to find him watching her.

'Ah, Sara. Marie tells me you are feeling much better, yes?' His low, warm voice was soothing. He wasn't still angry with her as she had feared, and she nervously smiled back at him.

'Yes, I really do feel very well. I've just eaten a huge breakfast. What day is it? I seem to have lost track of time.'

'Well,' he laughed softly, 'you have been here a week, and your "huge breakfast" was four hours ago!'

'Oh no! I can't have been here that long, surely?' She sat up in bed, distressed that she should have lost a week from her life, and not known it.

'Poor Sara, I'm afraid it has been a week. You really did need the rest, you know. However, you seemed so much better that I despatched the nurses yesterday, and the doctor tells me you are now quite well. He says there is no need for him to stay any longer, and he will leave today.'

'Doctor? Nurses?'

'Of course,' he said quietly. 'You needed professional nursing, and I felt it was necessary to have a doctor on hand.'

'Oh, Jabir! I—I'm so sorry to have been such a nuisance, I really am.' Sara was distressed. 'I'm so ashamed at all the trouble I've caused, I . . .'

'There is absolutely nothing for you to be sorry or ashamed about. If anything, it is I who . . .' He paused and put his book down on the table beside him. 'We must give thanks to Allah that you are now well again—there is nothing else that matters.' He stood up. 'I am going to leave you to rest and have your lunch. Please stay in bed today, and if you continue to feel well, we will have you up tomorrow.'

'Jabir . . .' Involuntarily, Sara put out her arms towards him. 'Please don't go. I—I . . .'

He looked at his pale, beautiful wife with her beseeching arms, and walked slowly over to the bed. He gazed down into her large blue eyes, swimming with tears, and at the curve of her full breasts revealed by her partially open silk dressing gown.

'Sara,' he sighed deeply, 'I should go and leave you to rest. The doctor has given me very strict orders not to tire you.'

She caught his hand. 'Please stay for a moment—please,' she pleaded. 'I'm so very, very sorry for—for everything. I . . .'

Jabir sat down beside her on the bed and removed a handkerchief from his pocket to wipe the tears which were falling from her eyes. 'We will have no more "I am sorrys" from you,' he said firmly. 'There is nothing for you to be sorry about, either now or in the past.'

He put his hand behind her head to support her, while he wiped away her tears. When he had finished, he pulled her gently towards him so she lay against his chest.

'There is a great deal of apologising and explaining to be done—by me. But later, when you are feeling stronger,' he said, as his hand slipped over the thin silk of her gown, gently stroking her back. 'But your first priority,' he told her, setting her back on the pillows, 'is to get really well—you understand?'

She nodded, then blushed deeply as he deftly pulled the sides of her gown together, adjusting her belt which had come loose.

'We can't have you giving the doctor any unprofessional ideas,' he said with a grin. Sara gave a small shaky gurgle of laughter.

'Now that is what I want to hear,' he said firmly. 'I want to hear laughter from you—there will be no more tears, promise me!'

'Yes, O Master,' she replied, with a slight grin.

'I said laughter—I didn't say cheek!' He flicked her nose with his forefinger. 'Now behave yourself, and rest.'

He stood up, his tall broad-shouldered figure towering over her. Sara ached with love, as she smiled mistily up at him. 'Are you going riding now?' she asked.

'I'm trying to school a particularly wild young stallion, so perhaps "riding" isn't the right word. I seem to spend more time sitting on the sand than I do in the saddle!' he said ruefully, walking over to the door. 'I will leave you to rest now.'

The next few days passed quietly. Jabir gave her a parcel sent by Hassa, now back from her Honeymoon. It contained several light silk caftans in glowing colours, and she was delighted to wear them as soon as she was up and about.

She spent her time quietly reading some books she had found in the library, and either lazing in the garden or in the sitting room at night. Always, Jabir was there, working on his papers or reading a book. She knew it couldn't last, but decided to leave the problems of the future until such time as she had to face them. For the moment she was just happy and content to be in his company.

They were sitting in the garden one night after dinner, drinking their coffee, when Jabir said, with a sigh, 'I can't really put it off any longer, Sara. I must tell you about my first marriage—about Miriam. I wish I didn't have to, but clearly I must.'

Sara felt a rising tide of panic. She had tried so hard to forget the dreadful three weeks which had followed the terrible scene in his room, the night of Hassa's wedding. She glanced over at him as he sat beneath a tree, whose leaves shaded his face from the moonlight, and her.

'Despite my father's divorce from his mother, Muhammed and I were good friends,' he began slowly. 'He was very wild, of course. His sexual exploits, for instance, were the talk of the French Riviera, and when he tried to break the bank at Monte Carlo, and failed, my father put his foot down. He told Muhammed that it was time he settled down, and that both he and I were to be married. My brother, as you can imagine, Sara, was furious, but my father held the purse-strings and there was nothing he could do.'

Jabir paused, as if to collect his thoughts. 'So, Muhammed was twenty-six and I was twenty-four, just having finished my education at Oxford and the Harvard Business School, when we were married to two sisters, the daughters of a Sheikh in the north of the country. The young girls were both very lovely, and I for my part was delighted with my bride.'

The harsh note in his low voice was painful to hear, and Sara, her hands clasped tightly together in her lap, braced herself to hear about his happy marriage and his lovely wife.

'Muhammed and Nurra's marriage was a disaster

from the start. He resented having to get married, and quickly returned to his old life of wine, women and aeroplanes. Nurra, virtually deserted, also soon realised that Muhammed would never be chosen to succeed my father, and feeling twice a loser, became a bitter woman.'

He sighed deeply. 'Yes, Sara, I was in love with my wife. Miriam was young and very lovely, and we had a long summer together after we were married. Unfortunately that autumn I had to travel abroad very extensively, and it meant leaving Miriam behind. She was by then expecting our first child, Nadia, so I arranged for her to stay with Nurra in an apartment of the old Palace.'

Jabir broke off his narrative to explain, 'The old Palace has been partially engulfed by the expanding town, and my father was in the process of building the new Palace, where we now live.'

Sara quietly murmured her understanding of the situation. She wished she could find a dark hole to crawl into, to escape from having to hear Jabir tell her how much he had loved Miriam. Filled with pain and anguish, she clasped her arms tightly about her body, forcing herself to listen as he resumed the story of his past life.

'I returned for Nadia's birth, of course, and then I had to go abroad again. Miriam did not apparently take to motherhood, and that was, I fear, when the trouble started.

'What I tell you now is not what I knew at the time, you understand. It seems that Miriam took to going out on her own, and would make for the bars which had sprung up to cater for the oil company employees. She would go with any man she could find, anyone who would give her what she referred to as "a good time".'

Sara couldn't believe her ears. She was absolutely bewildered by what Jabir was saying . . . all her fears, all her jealousy . . . She felt the painful knots inside her begin to loosen.

'Nurra,' he went on, 'jealous and unhappy herself, didn't discourage Miriam and certainly covered up for her in the beginning.'

'But I thought . . .'

'I know what you thought, Sara. My darling, you're such a sweet innocent—how could you be expected to tell the difference between truth, half truth and downright lies? Nurra . . . is Nurra, while as for poor Miriam, she was just a . . . a nymphomaniac.'

'Oh, Jabir!' she breathed in horror.

'Everyone knew about it, except her husband—the classic story! Eventually I found out, of course, but there was little I could do. There was trouble on our northern borders at that time, and my father needed the marriage alliance with her family. There could be no question of divorce, especially after the fiasco of Muhammed and Nurra's marriage.'

Jabir sighed deeply. 'We were locked together in an intolerable position. I—I couldn't touch her . . . I—I just buried myself in work and spent as much time abroad as I could. Poor little Mara—Allah may know who her father is, I certainly don't—but she is a sweet child, and I love her. After her birth, I had the children taken away and put into Scotty's loving care. Miriam was pleased, it saved her from having to make any effort to appear a good mother.'

Sara could have wept for him. She longed to put her arms around him and comfort him, but he was such a proud man that she didn't dare. She could only sit and listen as he exposed the raw wounds of his first marriage.

'Meanwhile, we had moved into the new Palace, and it was more difficult for Miriam to get in and out undetected. I came home in the middle of the day, unexpectedly, and found her in bed with one of the gardeners. I decided that that was the final straw. I threw him out, and locked her in her room before going to see my father.'

'Jabir!' cried Sara. 'Please don't distress yourself in going over this . . . Please!'

'The story is soon finished. I insisted she was sent back to her father, I could take no more. My father agreed, I divorced her, and she returned to her home in the north. Soon afterwards she drove her car straight into a heavy bus and was killed instantly.'

'I'm so sorry,' whispered Sara. 'So very, very sorry, Jabir. It's all my stupid fault that you've had to—to go over it all again. I'll . . . I'll never forgive myself for being so foolish—never!' she said as the tears fell down her cheeks.

He got up to come and sit beside her on the seat under the acacia tree. 'All that is in the past, Sara. It happened well over four years ago. I have had a long time to think things over, and to realise that it was simply a matter of picking a rotten apple from the barrel of life. It could happen to anyone.'

He put his hands on her shoulders, turning her to face him, as he looked down at her tear-stained face, clearly visible in the moonlight.

'It is very important for you—and me—that you clearly understand what I now say,' he said, as he softly kissed her trembling lips. 'I must tell you that there was no one else in my heart when I asked you to be my wife. After Miriam . . . after all I had been through, I did not believe it possible for me to love and trust anyone, ever again. It would have been, as you said, a terrible thing to do. To marry one woman when in love with another—terrible! Please believe me.'

'I do believe you, Jabir. I'm just so sorry that you've had such unhappiness with your first wife, and not a happier time with me. Truly sorry.' Sara sighed deeply, and hung her head in shame and distress.

'No, it is I who am truly sorry for all that has happened to you. It is all my fault. I should have told you about Miriam at the beginning, and then none of this—this agony for both of us would have happened.

'Now, my Sara, I know you have been unhappy at times with me. It has been difficult for you in a strange land—I do understand that. I also know that you were going to leave me in New York . . . yes? Who can blame you?' he added bitterly. 'However,' his voice softened, 'I—I would like us to try again. We have, I think, been happy here together, have we not? If you wish to leave me I will not stand in your way, you are completely free to go; but dear Sara, I—I would like you to stay.' His hands tightened as he looked intently down at her.

'I . . .' What could she say? Overjoyed as she was to know that he didn't still love Miriam, she knew he didn't love her either. Moreover, he had said nothing explicit about his relationship with Nurra. She ought to ask him about that, but she couldn't—she simply couldn't. The thought of the lies and heartbreaking unhappiness caused by that evil woman was more than she could cope with at this moment . . .

Jabir placed a hand gently under her chin and lifted her face towards him. 'Am I really so terrible, Sara?'

'Oh no! It's just that . . .' She raised her eyes to his. The naked desire he couldn't hide made her tremble, and as his face came nearer, and his lips found hers, she knew she was lost.

His mouth caressed hers, softly and gently, as he murmured, 'Please stay with me, my . . . my dear Sara.'

She eventually forced herself to break away from his embrace, and sat looking at her husband in the moonlight. She sighed deeply, knowing that there was only one answer for her, and dreading the unhappiness she could see in the years ahead.

'Yes, Jabir,' she said quietly. 'Yes, I'll stay with you.'

He gathered her gently into his arms. 'I will look after you, my Sara. I will make sure you are happy and content, I promise you.'

Just learn to love me, she prayed silently, as she lay quietly in his arms, looking at the stars in the night sky. Please, just love me.

CHAPTER TEN

SARA was wakened the next morning by the noise of what she thought of as her alarm clock—the arrival of the helicopter which flew down daily from the capital, with provisions and important papers for Jabir.

Jumping out of bed, she suddenly felt dizzy, as though the floor was coming up to meet her. A wave of nausea shook her slender body, and she stumbled into the bathroom.

Some moments later, Marie entered and cried with concern, 'Ah, *madame*! Are you all right?'

'Yes, Marie, I—I think so.' Sara stood leaning over the handbasin, as the waves of nausea receded. 'I just felt a little peculiar, that's all. It must be the fish we ate last night. I thought at the time that it wasn't maybe quite right.'

She splashed her face with cold water, and feeling much better, smiled at her worried maid. 'It's all right, Marie. I feel fine now—really.

'But please,' she said as she went back into her room, 'take away that breakfast tray, I really can't face it this morning.'

Sara looked at the ornately embroidered caftan Marie had put out on the bed. 'That's far too grand, Marie. I decided yesterday to do some gardening this morning, so I'll just wear some jeans and a cotton shirt.'

'Ah *non, madame*. Ze Prince, he tell me what you are to wear.' Her maid beamed at Sara with suppressed excitement.

'The Prince wants me to wear that dress? Marvellous, isn't it,' Sara grumbled as she complied with her husband's wishes. 'Men have no idea about clothes—absolutely none at all!'

She surveyed herself in the mirror. The sky blue silk caftan, with silver embroidery around the neck, reflected and enhanced the brilliant blue of her eyes.

'*C'est magnifique, madame.*' Marie looked fondly at her mistress.

'It may be—but it's hardly ideal for gardening!' Sara laughed, as she left the room through the french windows and walked across the garden. She could see Jabir's tall figure sitting under the acacia trees, and there seemed to be some people with him.

Surely ... it couldn't be ... she thought in bewilderment, and then as his companions turned at her approach, she gave a great cry of pleasure.

'Oh, Dad ... Dad!' she called, running down the path and into her father's arms. 'And Ann!' She went over to give her new stepmother a kiss. 'How fantastic to see you both here! When did you arrive? How long can you stay? ... Oh, Jabir,' she looked at her husband with starry eyes, 'how kind you are!'

'Sit down, Sara,' said Jabir with a wide smile, 'and let your poor parents finish their coffee. They had to be up at dawn to catch the helicopter, and are in need of refreshment.'

'How right you are, darling,' drawled Ann. 'Buzzing along in that little green bug, only inches away from the desert below. My God, I thought my last moments had come!' she shuddered dramatically.

'Rubbish!' Sara's father looked fondly at his wife. 'You enjoyed it no end. She persuaded that pilot chappie to let her have a go at the controls,' he confided to Sara and Jabir. 'That's when I thought *my* last moment had come, I can tell you!'

They all laughed and began talking happily together, as Sara caught up with her father and Ann's news.

'But Jabir kept your visit such a surprise,' Sara said. 'How long have you been out here in Assir?'

'Rather lost account of time,' said James Morrison, turning to Ann. 'About two days, isn't it, darling?'

'Just about, sweetie,' she smiled at Sara. 'I must say

your husband is the best thing to hit this family since sliced bread! Honestly, darling, what with being driven in a Rolls to Heathrow airport, private jet to Assir, and staying at your palace—a girl could get used to this life!' She turned to Jabir. 'Any more at home like you, darling? I'm not fussy—any age will do!'

Jabir gave a chuckle and raised her hand to his lips. 'My dear mother-in-law, I can see that I am going to enjoy your company immensely.'

'Oh God! That's cut me down to size. Mother-in-law indeed!'

They continued to talk for some time, until Jabir stood up. 'The day is beginning to get hotter now. Perhaps, Sara, you would like to show your parents to their rooms—everything has been prepared, and they can wash and rest. I unfortunately have some work to do, and will therefore see you all at lunch, yes?'

'Yes, Jabir—and thank you, thank you so much.' Sara gazed lovingly up at her husband, as he waved goodbye and walked away.

'Very sound fellow, that,' said James Morrison. 'Kind too. Couldn't do enough for us, could he, Ann?' He turned to Sara. 'I say, it's hot out here, what!'

'Yes, it is, but you'll soon get used to it. Come along and I'll show you to your rooms.'

An hour later Sara, sitting reading in the shade, looked up to see Ann, dressed in a scarlet caftan, walking towards her.

'Ann! You look splendid.'

'Well, so do you.' Ann looked at Sara's glowing skin and sparkling eyes. 'That nice girl Hassa lent me some of these caftans to wear; she sends you much love, by the way. I must say, I expected to see you all drawn and thin, at death's door, no less!'

'Oh—you know. You know about . . .'

'About you being taken ill and carted back here, etc.? Yes, darling, we do. Well,' Ann sat down on a chair beside Sara, 'as you can imagine, we started to get worried when after we'd had your cable from America, saying you were coming to see us, you never arrived.' Ann laughed. 'I must say your father was splendid— quite unlike his normal self! Telephone calls to New York, calls to the Assir Ambassador in London, threats to call in the Foreign Office—the lot! Anyway,' she continued, 'Jabir phoned from here and explained that you weren't well. "What have you done to my little girl, you bloody wog?" was one of the more polite things your father said to your husband! However, Jabir was very good and calmed him down in the end. He promised to fly us out as soon as you were well—and here we are.'

'Oh, Ann, I . . .'

'Darling, let's forget the whole thing. It's all over and done with, right? That palace of yours is very grand, isn't it, but I must say, this place has far more charm. I did tell you Hassa sent her love, didn't I? Super girl, and very funny. She gave me a complete and hilarious run-down on Assir in five minutes flat!'

'How are Scotty and the little girls?' asked Sara.

'Didn't see them, darling. Apparently while you were ill down here, Jabir flew up to the Palace and sent them off to join the King's hunting party. Hassa was very mysterious about the whole thing—very full of nods and winks which I totally failed to understand. However, it seems that Jabir had a long session with Hassa's mother, the Queen, before flying back to look after you; and the next day it was announced that a Princess Nurra was to marry some geriatric old prince.'

Sara's heart leapt, and she could hardly keep the joy out of her voice as she asked, 'Nurra's to be married? You're sure?'

'Darling, I've no idea who the lady is. All I know is that Hassa seemed very pleased about it—she kept laughing, actually, which struck me as a bit odd. I mean, this old prince, despite being very rich, lives in some tumbledown and ancient desert castle, miles from anywhere. It's full to the brim with dogs, hundreds and hundreds of them in every room, Hassa said. All stinking to high heaven, apparently—the dogs, I mean.'

Ann looked startled at Sara. 'Now you're laughing, just like Hassa—I don't think it sounds very funny—a fate worse than death, if you ask me!'

'Oh, Ann,' Sara laughed, 'you've made my day, you really have. What a case of rough justice!' and she started giggling again. 'Now,' she said, pulling herself together, 'what would you like to do while you're here?'

'As little as possible, darling. Your dear old dad and I are still trying to catch up on our jet-lag. Besides which, he's feeling just a tiny bit fragile, if you know what I mean. Living here in Assir, he's practically had to Sign the Pledge. The poor old boy can't seem to get a drink for love or money! By the way, he's got something to tell you, but maybe after lunch—he'll be more rested then.'

Sara spent the rest of the morning in a haze of happiness. Nurra's marriage, obviously engineered by Jabir, didn't really change anything between them. However, with Nurra removed from the scene, maybe their marriage would settle down, and maybe . . . maybe Jabir would come, in time, to love her as much as she loved him.

After lunch, Ann went to lie down, and Sara managed to catch Jabir before he returned to his office. 'It was such a lovely surprise, flying in Dad and Ann,' she said. 'You've been so kind to me, I . . . I'm very grateful.'

'But you should know, my Sara, that it gives me pleasure to please you.' Jabir drew her gently to him and smoothed the hair from her brow, running his finger down her cheek. 'You will recover faster with them around, yes?' He bent forward to kiss her gently, before disappearing inside his office. She returned to the sitting room to find her father pacing up and down with a haunted look on his face.

'Hello, darling,' he said, clearing his throat. 'I don't suppose there's any chance of a small snort? Little drop of the hard stuff? I'm . . . er . . . feeling a bit rough in this heat . . .'

'Oh, Dad!' Sara grinned. 'I suppose I'd better take pity on you. Let's see what we can find.'

'My God, that's more like it!' James Morrison settled back with a large whisky in his hand on a large, comfortable sofa, and gave a contented sigh. 'I know the fellows out here don't go for it, but without a glass or two of the old tincture, I don't think I'll survive!' He turned to look at his daughter. 'I must say, Sara, you look blooming. Ann was worried about you, after you got married, I mean. Insists I tell you what happened the day I sold the hotel—very insistent, she is.'

'We all know what happened, Dad,' Sara said quietly. 'There's no need to go through it all again.'

'I agree, Sara. Absolutely! However, the little woman's put her foot down, so I don't have a choice. I live under the cat's paw now, you know,' he added gloomily. 'Still, there you are . . .'

'I don't know where you are, Dad, but I'm lost. What is it you want to tell me?'

'About the sale, of course. Ann says I've got to—or else! So here goes. Now let's see. Yes, I'd just had breakfast—black coffee, actually—had a heavy time the night before, I recall. Anyway, got a message that the Arab johnny wanted to see me. So I toddled off, still feeling a bit fragile, if you get my meaning, and called in at his suite.

'Found he was a very pleasant fellow—spoke the Queen's English, for a start. So, I did my spiel: "Everything all right? Sorry about the bathwater—always a problem—come down and have a drink any time . . ." You know the sort of thing, Sara.'

'Oh yes, Dad!' Sara grinned. 'I remember well your magical touch with the guests. I used to have to spend hours soothing them down afterwards!'

'Now, Sara, don't be too hard on your old father.

Anyway, this chappie, your Jabir, he says, "Pull up a chair and pin back your ears"—or words to that effect. Nothing loath—still feeling rough—I settle down for a chat. Blow me if he doesn't say he wants to buy the hotel! Just like that! Took me a moment to get his drift, made him repeat what he'd said. Now, it was a very fair price. Actually it was bloody marvellous, at least twice what the hotel was worth. But I'd heard about all these oil-rich Arabs, practically own London nowadays. Wasn't sure I fancied the idea of adding our hotel to the list. Then blow me, he added the magic words, "after tax".'

James Morrison poured himself another whisky, and continued with his tale. ' "Well," I said, "break open the champers, you've got yourself a deal! No messing about, give me your pen and where do I sign?" I can be quick off the mark if I have to, you know, Sara.

'Then he continued—"Only on condition you give me permission to marry your daughter—no marriage, no sale". I blinked a bit there, you know. Said I didn't know you were both that friendly, but absolutely no problem. Happy to oblige—delighted, in fact!'

'Oh, Dad, I . . .' Sara suddenly felt depressed, remembering how she had fought against having to marry Jabir.

'Then suddenly the poor chap went to pieces. Bit embarrassing, actually, if you want to know. Obviously very emotional, these Arabs. Jumped to his feet and started pacing up and down the room, wringing his hands. Frankly, Sara, I thought he was touched in his works. Whole long speech about how he'd met you and suddenly, "wham", he's in love. Can't think of anything else, off his food, can't sleep, must have you as wife, etc., etc. You get the drift, I expect.'

'What!' Sara stared at her father, her mind in a whirl. 'You must have been mistaken.'

'Exactly what I said to him—my very words! I mean, you're a lovely girl, Sara, but as I said, "Hold hard a minute, laddie. You are sure it's my daughter you're talking about?" "Oh yes", he said, "blue eyes like sapphires, hair like golden rain . . ." and a whole lot more guff I've forgotten.

'So I said, "Calm down, my boy. No problem. You love her that much, you marry her—with my blessing! Roll out the champagne, bring on the dancing girls, etc." '

Sara sat looking at her father, totally unable to believe her ears. He must have been paralytically drunk at the time, she decided. There was no other explanation—none at all.

'Pathetically grateful, he was,' her father continued. 'Thanked me profusely, promised to shower you in diamonds, love and cherish you all his life, etc., etc. Frankly, darling, just the sort of rubbish that would normally make my hair curl. Still, when it's your only daughter—just what a father wants to hear, what?

'That's it, really. Can't think why Ann made such a fuss about me having to tell you all about it. He's a nice chap and I thoroughly approve of him. Knew you'd be happy—stands to reason you would. Fellow was dotty about you, wasn't he? Practically demented, in fact! This sort of thing gives a chap a thirst. I think I'll just have another small drop, if you don't mind?'

Totally bemused, Sara tried to bring some order into her chaotic thoughts. Her ears seemed to be pounding in a strange manner . . .

'Hello!' said her father. 'Sounds as if an aeroplane is landing.' They both got up and went into the garden. 'Thought so,' he said, 'it's a Hercules. Incredible planes, they can land anywhere.'

'But what's it doing here?' asked Sara, who felt she was swiftly losing touch with reality.

The large white gates of the Palace were thrown open, and in ran Nadia and Mara, followed by Scotty clucking like a broody hen. The children ran up and hugged Sara, both chattering at once. Sara, bending down to kiss them, heard her father say, 'I'm sure I know that chap's face . . .'

She stood up, and saw that the King was approaching with a smile. She was just about to go forward and greet him, when her father gave a bellow. 'It's Fruity! Old Fruity Shakir. Well, well! Haven't seen you for donkey's years. How are you, old boy? Whatever are you doing in this neck of the woods?'

'Oh God!' Sara moaned, shutting her eyes for a moment, and hoping the whole scene was a mirage.

'This I don't believe!' Jabir had left his office and stood beside her, with a wide grin, as they watched the two elderly men embrace.

'Sara, come and meet old Fruity. Haven't seen him since we were at Sandhurst together!'

'Dad!' she cried, trying in vain to catch his eye.

'Rum place this, Fruity,' he said, slapping the King's back. 'Can't get a drink anywhere! Do you remember the knees-ups we used to have at . . . what was the name of the pub?'

'The Goat and Compasses,' the King laughed, 'and I remember it well. How are you, James? You look in good health, I must say.' He put an arm around his old friend's shoulder. 'So you are Sara's father! Let's go and have a talk indoors, it's really too hot out here. How extraordinary—my son and your daughter . . .' and they disappeared into the Palace.

'For heaven's sake, what's happening?' Sara turned to ask Jabir, who was doubled up with laughter. 'It's like Grand Central Station in the rush hour!'

' "Fruity" indeed! I shall not let my father forget that in a hurry.' Jabir put his arm around her waist and kissed her cheek. 'Not only are you a delight to me, Sara, but I can see your family will also make sure that I never have a dull moment! Come on, let's see how they are both getting on.'

Sara climbed wearily into her bed that night, and looked back on what had been a quite amazing day. First there had been her father and Ann's arrival and then her father's story about the sale of the hotel to Jabir. I'm really worried about him, she thought in some distress. Maybe the amount of alcohol he must have consumed over the years was beginning to affect his brain.

Then, before she had been able to draw breath, there had been the King's arrival. That he and her father should be old friends—no one could have dreamt of such an extraordinary coincidence. The two men had spent most of the day reminiscing about old acquaintances, and the shouts of their laughter had filled the palace. The King, who had only intended to pay a fleeting visit to see how Sara was, had decided that he, Scotty and the little girls would stay the night. By the time dinner was ready, Sara had a splitting headache from all the noise and excitement.

Throughout the meal Jabir had kept an eye on the drooping figure of his wife, manfully trying to maintain an animated conversation with his father. As the meal finished, he rose and called for silence.

'As you know,' he said in a firm voice, 'my wife has not been well. I have decided, therefore, that as from tomorrow, Ann and Sara's father will join the King's hunting party in the desert, for a few days. Taking Scotty and the little girls with them, of course,' he added, looking his father firmly in the eye.

The King looked back at Jabir for a moment, then gave a slow smile. 'What an excellent idea, and one I should have thought of myself,' he said. 'Maybe you and Sara will join us later?'

'We'd love to,' she said, throwing a grateful glance to Jabir at the end of the table, before excusing herself and making for the sanctuary of her quiet bedroom. After today, she thought, as she slipped off to sleep, peace and quiet will be wonderful.

Getting out of bed next morning, she was assailed by a return of the sickness, and was retching violently in the bathroom when Marie brought in her morning tray.

'Ah, *madame*!' Marie cried. *'C'est sûr—vous êtes enceinte!'*

'I'm what?' muttered Sara, as she was struck by

another wave of nausea. 'Just leave me alone, please, Marie. I'll be all right.'

Marie disappeared, only to return shortly with Ann. They both helped Sara back into her room, and on to her bed to rest.

'Look, darling, this isn't really my sort of thing, but Marie says—if my French is correct—that you're pregnant.'

'Don't be silly, Ann,' said Sara weakly. 'I've just got a bug, that's all.'

Ann shrugged her shoulders and spoke hesitatingly in French to Marie, who left the room, coming back with Scotty in tow.

'Marie here tells me you've been sick for two mornings in a row, dearie,' Scotty said. 'I thought you might be expecting a baby as soon as I saw you yesterday. I can always tell, you know,' she said to Ann. 'It's something in the eyes. Oh yes, you're having a baby all right, dear,' she told Sara firmly.

'But I can't be!' wailed Sara. 'I just can't be!'

'Well,' said Nanny Scott, 'you know best what precautions you've been taking ... but I'll lay my life you're pregnant. About six weeks, I'd say.'

'Precautions? What precautions? I never thought ... I mean ... Oh God!' Sara rolled over to bury her head in the pillows.

Ann and Scotty looked at each other with troubled eyes.

'Come on, dearie,' the old nanny said bracingly. 'Master Jabir will be so happy, and so will the King. My word, you might have his first grandson—he will be pleased! It will be such a lovely time, and I'll look after you, there's no need to worry ...' Scotty was carried away with visions of her nursery being filled with babies once more.

'You don't understand,' Sara turned a tear-stained face towards the two women. 'It's an absolute disaster—an A1 unmitigated disaster!' and she buried her head again, weeping as though her heart would break.

CHAPTER ELEVEN

AFTER the mid-morning departure of their guests, Jabir announced that he had to visit some tribesmen, and would be away until the evening meal. Sara was grateful for the opportunity to be on her own, to try and absorb the new and major problem now facing her.

Wandering aimlessly about the small palace, sunk in thought, she came across a small hidden staircase off a narrow passage near her bedroom. It led to a small room with a cupola, like the domed glass roof of the pool, and was set invisibly behind the battlements of the Palace, containing a table, chairs and a bookcase.

Sara looked idly through the books, which were mainly old novels and biographies, many of which bore an inscription on the fly-leaf, 'Zahra de Vere', and then came upon an old photograph album. It had obviously belonged to Jabir's mother, and as Sara slowly turned the pages, she saw Zahra change from a gawky teenager into a lovely woman. Always laughing at the camera, her sheer joy of life came over so strongly that Sara's eyes filled with tears. To have been so happy and to have died so young—it was tragic.

There was a picture of her standing beside her husband that left Sara shaken—it was so like herself as to be almost a carbon copy. How strange that she, who looked so like Zahra, and had a name so similar, should have met Jabir and come to live in this Palace.

It wasn't as though Jabir had known his mother— Scotty had said he had never seen even a photograph of her, all of them having been destroyed by the King in his grief; all except the album in this hidden room. So it couldn't be excused away by the thought that he had a mother complex. It was just ... well, it was very strange.

It was the last photograph which held her attention. Jabir's mother was obviously very pregnant, as she stood looking lovely and very proud of the burden she carried. One hand held her husband's, while the other was placed over her long robe, as if to guard her unborn child.

Sara stared at the picture for a long time, and sighed. She had no choice but to stay with Jabir, and love him with all her heart, for ever. The photographs, the desert air, even the very walls of the building had always carried that message for her. It was only now that she heard it so clearly. She had tried to close her ears earlier that morning to Scotty's comforting words and Ann's good advice.

'It can be a shock the first time,' Scotty had said softly to Ann, as Sara wept on her bed. 'Some of my mums have been very emotional. Why don't you give me a few minutes alone with her. She'll be all right soon.'

'O.K., Nanny, you're the boss.' said Ann. 'Come on, Marie, let's leave Nanny Scott and your mistress alone for a bit.'

'Now, dearie,' said Scotty, when she and Sara were alone, 'cheer up—it's not the end of the world, you know.'

'Scotty, you don't understand . . .' Sara cried. She realised she couldn't tell the old nanny what a terrible blow to her the baby was. She was now committed for ever to Jabir, and she wept bitterly as Scotty tried to comfort her.

'Now, that's enough, dear,' Scotty spoke firmly. 'Go and wash your face, and then we'll do your hair and make you look more presentable. I don't know what's wrong, dear,' Scotty said as she rhythmically brushed Sara's long blonde hair. 'You've made my Jabir very happy. I brought him up, you know, after Miss Zahra died. Such a loving little boy, so thoughtful of others, always laughing.' She sighed. 'What a time he had with his first wife . . . you'd never credit it! He used to come and sit with me, not saying anything, just for comfort. He broke down and cried on my shoulder once, you know.'

'Oh no! ... I ...' Sara's heart was wrung with love and pain for her husband.

'Oh yes, he did. Terrible it was, a big grown-up man like him. He just slowly froze up inside—I could see it happening, and there was nothing I could do. My dear, he became so cold and hard, I used to worry about him so much. Then he married you and brought you here, and he's a different man. So much happier, and laughing too. I've watched him as he looks at you, his love—well, it just pours out of him. The fuss he makes if something isn't right for you ...!' She laughed. 'Well, just look at the way he's packing us all off into the desert, just so you can have some rest!'

'Scotty darling,' Sara said sadly, 'if only it was as simple as it sounds! Thank you for being so kind and sweet, I'll—I'll be all right now, really I will. Please don't say anything ... anything about the baby. Not yet, anyway.' She stood up. 'You must go and see to Nadia and Mara,' she said, giving Scotty a kiss. 'I'll be fine now, don't worry.'

'Well, if you're sure, dear ...?'

Left alone, Sara gave way to despair. If she were to be honest, there was nothing she wanted more than to have Jabir's child. But what about the future? *Committed.* The word seemed to echo in her head. Irrevocably committed by her love and now by the baby. Irrevocably committed to a husband who had no love for her.

Jabir was only thirty-two, and so—so very handsome. He was attracted to her at the moment, but without love, such attraction and desire would be bound to fade. What then? Some other Nurra, perhaps?

Ann came quietly into the room, to find Sara weeping silently.

'Sweetie,' she said, 'I don't know much about babies,

I'm pleased to say, but your reaction to being pregnant doesn't strike me as the usual one at all.'

'Oh, Ann, it's all such a ghastly mess! I don't know what to do, I really don't!'

'O.K. Let's calm down, and take this thing stage by stage, shall we? First of all, you're married to—I must say it—one of the most handsome and attractive men I've ever had the pleasure of meeting. You're going to have his baby, and yet here you are crying your eyes out. Why, Sara?'

Sara sighed. 'You remember when we got married . . .'

'Do I not!' Ann laughed, putting an arm around Sara's shoulder. 'I'm sorry, darling, but really it was an episode none of us is likely to forget.'

'Well, when we got married,' Sara continued in a small voice, 'I told Jabir that I didn't love him. He also said that he didn't love me. Love was, he said, "an unnecessary preoccupation of the Western mind". I remember the words perfectly. His . . . his feelings haven't changed since then.'

Ann looked at her stepdaughter's bowed head, the heavy curtain of her hair hiding her face from view. 'Do I take it,' she asked gently, 'that whatever Jabir may feel, your feelings have changed?'

Sara nodded silently.

'Well, I'm not surprised! Frankly, he's devastatingly attractive, absolutely yummy! However, I really can't believe that he doesn't find you desirable.'

'Oh yes,' Sara answered bitterly, 'he desires me all right. But he doesn't love me, Ann. Not me, as a person. I'm just a—a sexual object, someone he wants to go to bed with—that's all . . .' and the tears began to flow again.

'I'm sure you're wrong. I'm sure, in fact, that he cares for you very much. Surely your father has told you what Jabir said to him when he bought the hotel?'

'Oh, Ann, Dad must have been blind drunk at the time. There's no other explanation, none at all.'

'For heaven's sake, girl! There are worse fates than being married to the man you love, you know.'

'Not when he grows tired of amusing himself with me, and decides he fancies pastures new, there isn't. It's my idea of a living hell!' Sara groaned. 'I just don't know what to do.'

Ann sat looking quietly at her for a moment. 'My advice, for what it's worth, is that I think you and Jabir should have a long talk together. I have the very strong impression that neither of you has ever discussed your innermost feelings to each other. Don't you think it's about time you grew up, Sara, and did just that?'

'Ann! I thought you'd understand . . .' Sara looked at her father's wife in dismay.

'I do understand, Sara. I understand your position very well, and I've bags of sympathy for you. But, darling girl, you're going to have a baby, and that's not only a big responsibility, it's also Jabir's baby too—isn't it? You've simply got to talk things over with him, haven't you? Sitting here, crying your eyes out, won't solve anything.'

'You always give me such good advice, Ann,' Sara sighed. 'It's just that it's so hard to take, sometimes . . .'

'Here endeth the lesson for today!' Ann smiled at the unhappy girl. 'Buck up! Put some make-up on, and come and say goodbye to us all. Right?'

Ann's advice had been quite right, Sara thought, as she looked again through the old photograph album which had belonged to Jabir's mother, all those years ago. Maybe . . . maybe she would be able to find the courage to talk to Jabir about her feelings, but she didn't feel able to do it yet. However, she'd certainly have to tell him about the baby soon. As Ann had so rightly pointed out, it was his baby too.

She really had no other choice than to love and cherish Jabir with all her heart. Her own innate honestly compelled her to admit that she wasn't able, in fact, to do anything else. Quite simply, a life without Jabir was not a life worth living. Her only doubts had been in facing the future, which held such unhappiness for her.

Sara and Jabir had a quiet dinner together that night. After coffee in the garden, as usual, he insisted that she had an early night. 'It has been an exhausting two days for you, my Sara. You must have a long lie-in tomorrow, and recover your strength, yes?'

'It was lovely to see Ann and Dad, but when your father turned up—well, there certainly was a lot of noise and excitement,' she laughed softly. 'Still, I'm looking forward to joining them all at the desert camp—it sounds such fun!'

'But only when I feel you are well enough to go,' Jabir said firmly, helping her to rise from the bench.

'You mustn't wrap me in too much cotton wool,' she smiled up at him. 'I'm becoming thoroughly spoiled!'

'I hope so!' His voice thickened, as he drew her slowly towards him. 'I promised to cherish you, and I intend to do just that, my Sara.' His kiss was soft and gentle, and she felt her body respond to the piercing sweetness of his lips.

'Come,' he said at last, taking a deep breath to steady himself, 'I must take you back to your room immediately, or I shall do something I shall undoubtedly regret!'

Despite all that had happened that day, Sara found she was unable to sleep. Jabir's kiss had disturbed any equilibrium she had managed to assume. She longed for his touch, and ached for his passionate embrace.

Ashamed of her urgent need for him, and for the love he couldn't give her, she was in torment. She tried to read, but that didn't stop her feverish thoughts and she tossed and turned on her bed in misery.

It was all too much, and she gave up the struggle to sleep and sat in the chair by the window. Maybe it's because it's such a hot night, she thought—and knew that she wasn't fooling herself. She, quite wantonly, needed him. Even if he didn't love her, she needed him. Tears of shame came to her eyes, as she left the chair and paced up and down her room. She must cool down, somehow. Maybe a cold bath . . .?

Of course, she told herself—the little pool. Why not? If she was very quiet, Jabir would never know she was there. She collected a large towel from her bathroom and quietly opened the small door which led to the pool.

The moonlight streaming in from the glass roof lit the still water, leaving the sides and the paintings in darkness. Sara walked silently to the edge and pinned her hair up on top of her head, before slipping off her gown and sliding silently into the water. It was wonderfully cool and she swam around for a while before turning over to float on the water, gazing at the stars she could see through the roof.

Time seemed to stand still as she gently floated, her body bathed in the silver light of the moon's beam. Eventually, feeling much better and relaxed, she stepped out and dried herself. She had just put on her nightgown when she heard a small sound and looked around in the darkness, startled.

'It's only me, Sara,' said Jabir softly. 'I couldn't sleep either—it's such a hot night. I was just sitting here in the corner after having a swim, when you came in.' His disembodied voice came from the darkness, across the other side of the pool.

'Oh,' she said, nervously backing away from his voice. 'You made me jump.'

'I'm sorry,' he said, walking slowly towards her. 'I didn't mean to spy, but,' his voice thickened as he came nearer, 'but you looked so lovely in the moonlight, that I . . . I had to stay and watch you.'

They stood together in the dark for a long moment, before he slid his hands gently around her waist and down on to her hips to pull her against his body, clothed in a silk dressing gown.

Sara stood as if in a trance, feeling the warmth of his body through the thin layers of silk. He slowly kissed her eyes, before letting his mouth trail over the shell of her ear, and slide down the curve of her neck. His lips teased and tantalised her, as shivers of delight danced across her skin to send tremors of desire through her body.

'You know why you couldn't sleep . . .?' he whispered in her ear, as his fingers very slowly slipped the thin straps of her gown off her shoulders, and down her arms. 'Why neither of us could sleep?'

Her gown rustled to the floor as he removed the pins from her hair, to let it fall, before his hands slid slowly down her back and began to gently caress the swell of her hips.

'Why can't you sleep, Sara . . .?' he murmured, as his mouth teased hers, in a provocative and tender kiss. She slid her arms around his neck, burying her hands in his hair, and pressed herself to him. He trembled and groaned with desire as he felt her cool body so close to his.

'Because I want you—so much,' she moaned softly in his ear. 'Oh, Jabir, I . . . I want you to make love to me.' She was totally in the thrall of such a surge of passion that she couldn't have stopped herself saying the words, even if she had wanted to.

'Aha!' With a great shout of triumph he lifted her up in his arms. 'At last!' He bore her, as if she was thistledown, into his bedroom and placed her gently on his bed. 'Oh, my lovely Sara—at last you've told me what I want to hear!' His voice was thick with passion as he lay beside her, his hands caressing her body, before he caught her to him and groaned again, as he tasted the sweetness of her breasts. ·

And then she was lost, as always, in some deeply passionate mist as their two bodies became as one in the stillness and the silence of the desert night.

The early morning sun woke her, and her heart sang as she realised that Jabir hadn't left her side during the night. Instead, she was lying clasped in his arms, her cheek against his warm chest.

Listening to the steady beat of his heart, she moved instinctively and languorously against his hard firm body, as erotic images of his lovemaking the night before flooded her mind. Surely Jabir must guess soon how much she loved him? The very abandonment of her response to his sensual touch would make discovery a certainty before long.

Jabir's eyes had opened at her movement, and his strong brown arms tightened possessively about her, as he ran his mouth gently over her face. He kissed her eyelids, whispering softly in Arabic, before he found her soft lips tremulously waiting for his possession.

The tantalising sweetness of his kiss as he explored the softness of her mouth caused a sudden surge of desire to run through Sara, her hands moving to stroke and caress Jabir's long, lithe body.

'Ah . . . Sara!' A deep shudder ran through his frame at the urgent touch of her soft fingers. He slowly withdrew his mouth to raise his head and look down at her beautiful face. Sara's brilliant blue eyes, shining with desire, gazed back at him, her small pink tongue nervously flicking over her softly parted lips, as she felt the increasing urgency of his body.

'Oh, my love,' he said softly. 'Last night you told me, of your own volition, what I've been waiting so long to hear you say. Oh, my darling Sara, how I . . . how I love you! Only Allah knows how much I love you,' he cried as he rained fervent kisses on her face.

'Wha . . .' Sara's startled cry was stopped by the descent of his firm mouth on hers, and for a few moments she was powerless to do anything but respond to his mounting ardour.

Jabir's lips slowly abandoned hers to move down her throat, towards the soft swell of her aching breasts, as she slowly surfaced from a deep mist of ecstasy. 'What . . . what did you just say?' she gasped, as his tongue teased the swollen rosy tips. 'No! Please, Jabir . . .' she cried as she felt her body respond to his intimate touch.

Desperately, she pushed against his hard body. 'Please, Jabir, what did you just say?'

He raised his head, and looked tenderly down at his lovely wife.

'My darling,' he said, 'I love you. I love you so much that I—I cannot keep silent any more. I cannot stop myself. I—I must tell you how much I love you.' He groaned, 'I cannot make love to you, and not say how much I love and worship you.'

Sara gave a resounding peal of joyous and slightly hysterical laughter. 'For heaven's sake! Why did you never tell me? Why keep silent?'

'I was . . . I was frightened of . . . Damn it, Sara!' he cried, 'getting you into bed was hard enough! I thought if you knew I loved you as well, it would all be too much.' He lowered his head to give her a deeply passionate kiss. 'Please, my love, I didn't and still don't want to frighten you. You might come to love me, in time. It's not impossible. I think . . .'

'The trouble with you, Jabir, is that you think too much!' Sara returned his kiss with fervour. 'When I think of all the weeping I've done because you didn't love me. Oh, my darling Jabir, you great fool! How can you hope to rule this country, when you don't even know how much your wife loves you!'

'Truly, Sara?' He looked stunned, and fell back on the pillows, almost unable to believe what he heard. 'You do truly love me?'

'Of course I do. I've loved you practically from the beginning, but I didn't realise you loved me too. Oh, my darling, what fools we've been! What stupid fools!' Sara sat up in the bed, bouncing with excitement, only to be immediately assailed by a sudden surge of nausea.

'Oh no!' she groaned, and quickly swung her legs off the bed, dashing for his bathroom.

'My dearest love, what's wrong?' Jabir asked anxiously, as he helped to sponge her white face.

'Well, it's not your damn yacht this time!' she tried to

joke, as another spasm of sickness racked her slim frame.

'Ah . . .' he said, comprehension dawning as her nausea faded and he eased her into one of his towelling robes, before leading her gently back to his bed.

'I—I'm going to have a baby,' she said, looking up at him nervously, as he sat beside her, gently swabbing her forehead with a cold flannel. 'You don't mind . . .?'

'Mind?' he laughed. 'My darling girl, I am absolutely delighted! I told you once there were two major things you hadn't thought of, and one was having a baby.'

'And the other?' she asked.

'My loving you, of course!'

'You're wrong, Jabir. I've thought of nothing else for so long. But you told me in London that you didn't love me, that love was—how did you put it?—a preoccupation of the Western mind.'

'My dear girl, you've no idea what turmoil I was going through at the time.' He looked seriously at her for a moment. 'You walked into my suite at your father's hotel and—I can't even begin to explain it— suddenly I was in love. Me! A widower with two children! Violently and helplessly in love: Wham— pow—splat! Just like those dreadful comics!' He drew a deep breath. 'You can't possibly conceive how it was, Sara. To begin with, I felt such a fool. I couldn't believe what was happening to me, and at my age too! I found myself behaving just like a young teenager; off my food, I couldn't sleep, never able to think about anything else but your lovely face—it was dreadful and wonderful, all at the same time.' He gave a dry bark of laughter.

'As you can imagine, I fought against it—only Allah knows how hard I tried. For two long weeks I did everything I could to rid my mind of your image—it was all hopeless. My business dealings went completely to pot. My dear, I still shudder at some of the decisions I made at that time! Eventually I gave up the struggle. I knew I had to have you. Not just sexually, you understand, although you are very, very desirable.' He paused to kiss her again and again. *I had to possess you, totally.*

'I—I was terrified of you.' Sara smiled lovingly at him. 'I didn't realise it was because I was attracted to you. All I knew was that you made me feel most peculiar . . .' She laughed and smoothed his hair back, lightly kissing his ear.

'I could see that—I knew you were terrified of me, and it is that which has led to all my mistakes. You were quite right, I did blackmail you and your family——but, darling, I was out of my mind, quite insane. I had to possess you, in order to love and cherish you. Nothing else mattered. Nothing!'

'My father told me about it, when he was staying here last week. Oh, Jabir,' she laughed, 'I thought he had been blind drunk at the time, but I was maligning him. Poor Dad!'

'I knew I frightened you. When you told me you didn't love me—of course I told you I felt the same way. What else was I to do? And then I frightened you further on the boat, and . . .' he shuddered, 'I didn't know what to do. Everything I did made you more and more nervous.'

'Oh, darling, if only I'd known!' she sighed.

'We were both fools—you were right, Sara. But consider my problem. I knew, quite simply, that I would go mad if I didn't make love to you, and I was sure that you were sexually attracted to me. What was I to do? That first night here, when I came into the bedroom and saw you lying asleep, looking so very beautiful—I couldn't help myself. I had to express my love for you, I just had to!' He clasped her tightly in his arms. 'It was so wonderful, our lovemaking, that I couldn't have left you alone after that, even if I'd tried. I thought that if I came at night and proved to you how passionate you were . . . you really are such a passionate woman, Sara!' He smiled, as she blushed. 'I also thought that if I left before you woke, and never gave you the chance to be embarrassed about it . . . you are also a very proud woman, my love . . . you might come to love me in the end.'

'*So that was why . . .*'

'It's all over now, but I nearly killed myself that night, when you repeated Nurra's lies.' He sighed.

'It's all over now, Jabir. We love each other deeply, that's all that matters, surely?' Sara kissed him gently.

'Yes, my dearest, dearest wife,' he said, burying his face in the fragrant cloud of her hair.

'You really are pleased about the baby?'

'My darling, how can you doubt it?' He smiled, and placed a gentle hand on her stomach. 'My son . . .' he said happily. 'You wonderful, wonderful woman! Now, I must get you some tea and a dry biscuit. You'll feel better soon, I promise you.'

'Oh, Jabir,' Sara laughed weakly, as he went to the door and called for Hamid, 'it may be a girl, you know.'

'Nonsense!' he grinned, returning to her from having given his orders. 'You, my beloved Sara, are going to give me a tribe of boys—and just think how pleasurable it will be for us to create them. *Wallahi*,' he kissed her passionately, 'I am a lucky man!'

'What an Arabian chauvinistic pig you are today!' she said with a smile, as she lay contentedly in his arms until Hamid returned with the tray.

'I shall ignore such a disrespectful remark.' Jabir's eyes gleamed with amusement. 'However, talking about my Arab characteristics does remind me that there are—er—one or two things I should discuss with you. One or two—er—matters that need clarifying, one might say.'

Sara, sitting up in bed, looked over at her husband as he sat in a chair by the window, nervously fiddling with his teaspoon. Knowing that he loved her made her feel supremely confident. 'One might say,' she smiled gently, 'that perhaps Nurra needs some clarification . . .?'

'I was, in fact, thinking of something else, which we

will come to in a moment. However, you are right, there is the matter of Nurra.' He sighed. 'I had seen very little of her, you know, until my brother was killed. I had to return to Assir to support my father in his grief, and sort out Muhammed's affairs. My poor father leant on me considerably at the time, Sara, and I suppose it became obvious that I was the person most likely to succeed him on the throne.'

Jabir leant back in his seat, staring at the ceiling. 'As you can imagine, my love, the pressures on me to marry Nurra were heavy ones to resist. It made sense politically, and would have been a tidy solution to what had been a most unfortunate situation. However, as time went by, I found it more and more difficult to comply with my father's wishes.

'How can I explain it? Nurra was beautiful and clearly wished to marry me, but still I hesitated. Not because I cared for anyone else, but because I came to see that it wasn't myself as a person she valued, but chiefly what she saw as the power and position that I, as a possible future king, could confer on her and her family.'

He gave an unhappy laugh. 'It is not, of course, unusual for people who marry for reasons of state to cordially detest each other. However, I had, as you know, just been through one unhappy marriage, and I certainly did not want another. So I hesitated . . . prevaricated . . .'

'Jabir darling! You really don't have to . . .'

'Oh yes, I do, Sara. Not only is confession supposed to be good for the soul, but in this case I really did not behave at all well. To be frank, I didn't say "yes" and I didn't say "no". Of course I wished to please my father, of whom I am very fond, but I couldn't quite bring myself to go through with the marriage. It is not an episode that reflects any credit whatsoever upon myself. However, I met and married you, and that was that.'

'She was so beautiful and sophisticated that I couldn't see how you could resist her. When I saw you leaving her house one night—well! I was terribly jealous of her, you know,' Sara confessed, her face pink with embarrassment as she gazed down into her teacup.

'I cannot recall . . . ah yes. We had been dancing, had we not? She telephoned with some stupid rigmarole about an important paper of my brother's—I can't remember what. I do know I felt very angry with her at the time. I had been busily trying to seduce you—rather successfully, I thought—when . . . Oh Sara,' he laughed, 'I love to see you blush!' He gazed tenderly at his beautiful wife. 'In fact, my darling,' he said, coming over to sit beside her, 'your response was so ardent that I—well, I nearly lost all control of myself. I was astounded to find that it was you who was seducing me!'

'I didn't!' she protested, a tide of deep crimson spreading over her face. 'It was . . . it was the way you were kissing me . . .'

'How did I kiss you? I've forgotten. Was it like this . . .?' he whispered, as his mouth possessed her soft lips, and there followed a long silence, only punctuated by occasional soft murmurs in Arabic.

'Jabir! You're insatiable!' Sara gasped, as she struggled to sit up, trying to look sternly at the husband she loved so much.

'Yes,' he agreed simply, with a wicked grin. 'I hope you will feel able to complain about it for a long time to come!'

'Now, Sara,' he said, stopping her giggles with a firm kiss, 'I give you my word that I did not, at any time, make—er—make love to Nurra. What she was hoping to achieve, with her lies and half truths, was apparently that either we would become so estranged that I would divorce you; or that you would, in turn, become so unhappy as to leave me. It makes me quite ill to think how nearly she succeeded. Although why she thought I would turn to her, when I had lost you, Allah alone knows!'

He gave a deep sigh. 'Maybe if you and I had been

more honest with each other, or if we had talked more together, much of the unhappiness she caused need never have happened.' He made a dismissive gesture. 'So much for Nurra and the past. Her future need not concern us.'

'You—you were a bit ruthless there, my darling,' she said. 'I heard from Hassa, via Ann, of poor Nurra's fate.'

'Nurra made two classic errors, Sara,' he said in a hard voice. 'She attempted to interfere in my life, and, more importantly, she hurt you. Neither is forgivable. Now, I am tired of talking about that stupid woman. We will discuss her no more.'

'Yes, O Master!' Sara gave a gurgle of laughter.

'Sara!' he said with exasperation, then his face relaxed, and he smiled back at her. 'I was being imperious again, wasn't I?'

'Well, to be frank—we are being frank with each other, aren't we?' she gently teased him, as she peeped at her husband from beneath her lowered lashes. 'The answer is, yes—you were.'

'Ah, my darling,' he smiled fondly at her, 'I can see that you will be very good for me. Whether I shall always appreciate your frankness—that is another matter.' He took a deep breath. 'Now, this is where I want you to listen very carefully. It is important for both of us that you understand me clearly, yes?'

Sara nodded silently.

'I had a long talk with my father when you were ill, and another session with him the night he stayed here. I told him that I was tired of his indecision regarding myself. I was weary of trotting around the globe, making business deals, when there was so much work to do here. Such an existence is not, moreover, conducive to a happy married life. I desire the opportunity to serve my country in the coming years, and to do so I must have a firm position, here in Assir. I demanded that he made me his heir immediately.'

'What did he say?'

Jabir laughed wryly. 'He asked me why it had taken me so long to talk to him about it. "I was getting worried about you, my boy" is what he actually said! So next week it is to be announced, and possibly Fahad, Hassa's brother, will be trained for my old job.'

'I am pleased for you,' Sara said slowly. 'You will make a good king when the time comes.'

'I pray to Allah that it may be so,' he replied. 'As we will be living mainly in Assir, I also insisted that we had our own private palace, away from the city. I have chosen a site by the sea shore, which is near enough to the centre of things and yet is surrounded by the desert you love so much.'

'Jabir, I . . '

He ignored her interruption as he went on. 'As I said, we'll be living here in Assir, but of course, I intend that we shall travel abroad for pleasure, as and when we wish.'

He paused, and took a deep breath. 'Now, Sara, I hope and pray that you will approve of my actions. I have done what I can to make our life as comfortable as possible for you. Nurra is gone, and there will be a new palace—yours. I suspect that you do not relish the thought of being Queen in the future, but I would protect you and help as best I can. Yes?'

'Oh, Jabir,' she threw her arms about his neck, 'I'm really very happy with your arrangements. There is just one thing, though . . .'

'Anything! Anything your heart desires.'

'Well—er——' She hid her face in his shoulder. 'My heart desires,' she murmured, 'that we should no longer have separate bedrooms. I was so unhappy,' she said, lifting her face to his, 'so terribly unhappy when you used to disappear every morning before I woke, and . . .'

'My love,' he laughed happily, 'we will share only one room with the largest bed I can find—I promise!

'Sara,' he murmured a few moments later, 'are you feeling better now?'

'Yes, much better, really.'

'That is good,' he said, as he slowly began to undo her robe. 'Because I have an urgent need to make love to you.'

'Darling Jabir,' she laughed happily, as she placed her arms around his neck, nuzzling his cheek. 'Don't you ever think of anything else?'

'As far as you are concerned, my adorable wife,' he said firmly, as his hands began to caress her soft body, 'the answer is "*never*"!'

Coming Next Month in Harlequin Presents!

703 THE WALL   Amanda Carpenter
A lonely Lake Michigan shore seems an unlikely place for a
tormented reclusive writer to meet a beautiful singing star. But
meet—and love—they do, in this passionate and sensitive
romance.

704 DARK PARADISE   Sara Craven
For special reasons of her own, a young woman feigns interest in a
crusading journalist and accompanies him to the West Indies—
where events change her pretend love to the real thing!

705 DANCE WHILE YOU CAN   Claire Harrison
A dedicated dancer doesn't have room in her life for love *and*
career. So thinks a lovely Manhattan prima ballerina—until a holiday
affair with a handsome businessman wreaks havoc with her
philosophy.

706 SHADOW MARRIAGE   Penny Jordan
Deep in their hearts, an estranged husband and wife, both a part of
Hollywood's glamorous film industry, know they need to reconcile
to find happiness...yet cruel Fate seems to have other plans.

707 ILLUSION OF LOVE   Patricia Lake
An intriguing tale of romance, jealousy and passion that sweeps
from a beautiful South Pacific island to an English manor by the
sea, and culminates on a luxurious yacht on the French Riviera.

708 GOING UNDERGROUND   Karen van der Zee
When a taxing career pushes her to the edge, a young woman
spends two months in Virginia helping a handsome single parent
with his son. In so doing she discovers her inner strength...and
capacity for love.

709 IMPRUDENT CHALLENGE   Jessica Steele
A plucky English miss visits her suddenly bankrupt father in Japan
to delve into the cause of his financial crisis—only to find herself
falling for the very man responsible for it!

710 THE INHERITANCE   Kay Thorpe
When an English girl inherits a ranch in Florida, she travels there
with the intention of selling...but when she meets, and dislikes on
sight, the arrogant would-be buyer, she quickly changes her mind.

Harlequin Photo Calendar

Turn Your Favorite Photo into a Calendar.

JULY 1984

The Browns

Uniquely yours, this 10x17½" calendar features your favorite photograph, with any name you wish in attractive lettering at the bottom. A delightfully personal and practical idea!

Send us your favorite color print, black-and-white print, negative, or slide, any size (we'll return it), along with **3** proofs of purchase (coupon below) from a June or July release of Harlequin Romance, Harlequin Presents, Harlequin Superromance, Harlequin American Romance or Harlequin Temptation, plus $5.75 (includes shipping and handling).

- -

Share the joys and sorrows
of real-life love with
Harlequin American Romance!™

GET THIS BOOK
FREE as your introduction to
Harlequin American Romance —
an exciting series of romance
novels written especially for
the American woman of today.

Mail to:
Harlequin Reader Service

In the U.S.
2504 West Southern Ave.
Tempe, AZ 85282

In Canada
P.O. Box 2800, Postal Station A
5170 Yonge St., Willowdale, Ont. M2N 5T5

YES! I want to be one of the first to discover
Harlequin American Romance. Send me FREE and without
obligation *Twice in a Lifetime.* If you do not hear from me after I
have examined my FREE book, please send me the 4 new
Harlequin American Romances each month as soon as they
come off the presses. I understand that I will be billed only $2.25
for each book (total $9.00). There are no shipping or handling
charges. There is no minimum number of books that I have to
purchase. In fact, I may cancel this arrangement at any time.
Twice in a Lifetime is mine to keep as a FREE gift, even if I do not
buy any additional books.

Name _____ (please print)

Address _____ Apt. no.

City _____ State/Prov. _____ Zip/Postal Code

Signature (If under 18, parent or guardian must sign.)

This offer is limited to one order per household and not valid to current Harlequin
American Romance subscribers. We reserve the right to exercise discretion in
granting membership. If price changes are necessary, you will be notified.
Offer expires December 31, 1984   154 BPA NAVJ

AMR-SUB-1